What She Left Behind

What She Left Behind

Tracy Bilen

Simon Pulse
NEW YORK LONDON TORONTO SYDNEY NEW DELHI

SIMON PULSE

An imprint of Simon & Schuster Children's Publishing Division

1230 Avenue of the Americas, New York, NY 10020

First Simon Pulse paperback edition May 2012

Copyright © 2012 by Tracy Bilen

All rights reserved, including the right of reproduction in whole or in part in any form.

SIMON PULSE logo and colophon are registered trademarks of Simon & Schuster, Inc.

For information about special discounts for bulk purchases, please contact Simon & Schuster Special Sales at 1-866-506-1949 or business@simonandschuster.com.

The Simon & Schuster Speakers Bureau can bring authors to your live event.

For more information or to book an event contact the Simon & Schuster Speakers Bureau at 1-866-248-3049 or visit our website at www.simonspeakers.com.

Designed by Mike Rosamilia

The text of this book was set in Adobe Caslon Pro.

Manufactured in the United States of America

2 4 6 8 10 9 7 5 3 1

Library of Congress Cataloging-in-Publication Data

Bilen, Tracy.

What she left behind / Tracy Bilen. — 1st Simon Pulse pbk. ed.

p. cm.

Summary: Sixteen-year-old Sara's mother goes missing before she and Sara can move to a new town to escape Sara's physically abusive father.

ISBN 978-1-4424-3951-1

[1. Family violence—Fiction. 2. Fathers—Fiction. 3. Missing persons—Fiction.] I. Title.

PZ7.B4924Wh 201   [Fic]—dc23   2011028989

ISBN 978-1-4424-3952-8 (eBook)

What She Left Behind

CHAPTER 1

Monday

I sometimes have this dream that I'm drowning in a giant bowl of oatmeal. That's how I feel when I'm at home. When I'm at school, it's different. I hang out with Zach, sneak Ritz Bits crackers during class, and read horror novels in history. I like horror because it puts things in perspective. I mean, at least I'm not being chased by killer bees and no one's trying to hack off my arm.

First period is band. Right now it's marching season, which sucks because it's all about football. I hate football. Usually I stuff a copy of *Soap Opera Digest* between my uniform and my real clothes so I have something to do between the pregame and halftime shows.

What I really like is concert season. That's when I get to trade in my big, clunky, ordinary clarinet for my E-flat clarinet. Matt—that's my brother—used to call it the "shrunken clarinet," as if I had left it in the dryer too long.

I'm playing my shrunken clarinet in the living room, trying to chase away that oatmeal-dream feeling, when my mom comes in and stands right next to me. "Sara, we have to go," she whispers, even though my dad isn't there to hear her. She's not crying. She's calm. Matter-of-fact. As if she's asking me whether I want mayo or mustard on my sandwich. Except in secret.

I know it's time to go. I've known for a long time.

"You must think I'm an idiot for not getting us out of here sooner."

"It's okay," I say. I twirl my ponytail, like you do to turn off the faucet when the hose is spraying all over you. I do that when I'm nervous. Or lying. Or both. "I'll go get my things." I open the case and put away my clarinet.

"We'll leave at lunch tomorrow. I'll pick you up at the Dairy Dream."

Tomorrow? When you decide to do something, you should just do it. Otherwise you might change your mind. Especially if you're my mom.

"Don't pack a lot. Just your duffel bag."

One bag? How do you put a whole life in one bag?

"Leave it under your bed. I'll stop and get it just before I come pick you up."

That's it? This is Mom's plan?

"Hurry. Before he gets home."

On your marks, get set . . .

"Sara, we have to be careful. Your dad said—"

"Can't we talk later? Like, tomorrow in the car?" I know what she wants to tell me. She forgets I was there.

* * *

We were in the living room. Dad was reading a book about the history of polio. He always reads nonfiction. I was at the piano, playing a song called Wildfire *by ear and trying to remember the words. My mom was dusting. She knocked a book off a shelf and it hit the ground with a loud bang.* Like a gunshot.

"What Matt did is your fault," *my dad said, slamming his book shut.* "And don't you ever forget it!"

I stopped playing. Before I took my next breath, he was across the room. Dad cupped his hand around Mom's throat and slammed her head into the wall. Thump!

Mom didn't fight back. She never did. The worst part is, she didn't look afraid. She just looked empty.

I stared, like always. A tree in the Petrified Forest. I looked down at my hands and feet and ordered them to move, only they wouldn't. Please don't let her die. Please, Matt, tell God to let her live.

"*Don't even* think *of leaving.*"

Slam! *The wall again.* "Do you hear me? Don't even *think* of it. I won't have people saying, 'You know that Ray guy? Heard what his son did? Yeah, well, his wife left him too.'"

Let her go, let her go! *my voice said inside me, only my mouth wouldn't open so the words couldn't get out.*

Dad wrapped one hand around her chin and forced her to look at him. "I will find you," *he whispered.* "Guaranteed."

He let go of her and took the Statue of Liberty figurine that we got a long time ago on vacation off the shelf. He threw it against the wall, next to Mom's face. It shattered on impact.

Later I picked up the big pieces and vacuumed up the rest. Dad was back to reading. He smiled sweetly as if nothing had happened. "Thanks, Sara. You always know the right thing to do without being asked."

Trying to forget that day, I hurry down the hallway to my room. I pull my duffel bag from the closet. It's red and black, and has the logo of a cigarette company on it. My dad smokes so many cigarettes that he's in some kind of rewards program. Our whole house smells like cigarettes, only once you're inside for a few minutes you can't tell anymore. *In a few days I'll be living in a place without that smell.*

I open the zipper and shove Sam, my stuffed dog, inside. Sam has brown fur and a box-turtle-size black patch on his back. He also has a gaping hole in his neck, but the stuffing is so solid it never falls out. I know it's stupid to take him. At sixteen, no one should need a stuffed animal. Too bad I have trouble sleeping without holding on to him.

After Sam, I add my shrunken clarinet to my bag. Technically it's not mine—it belongs to the school—but I can't leave it behind. Not only is it cute-looking, but you can play amazingly high notes on it. Somehow I'll figure out a way to pay for it. I'm going to need it to keep me from obsessing about my dad showing up and dragging us back to life in the oatmeal bowl.

Next I pack the usual—underwear, socks, jeans, T-shirts. I tuck in a few sparkly silver butterfly clips and my Sheer Blonde shampoo and conditioner, for my hair that's still sort of blond and that I desperately want to stay blond. My blondness links me to my brother and my mom. My dad's hair is brown, and I want no part of looking or being like him.

Should I pack for winter, too? I throw in my Eastern Michigan sweatshirt, then switch it out for something more generic. No sense broadcasting where we're from—Mom and I will need to blend in to our new town.

Since Mom has me packing just a duffel bag, she's probably planning on getting us new stuff. Although I'm not sure how. Has she been hiding cash in the freezer, next to the waffles my dad never touches? The only credit card I've ever seen her use is the one with Mickey Mouse on it—not because we're ever going to go to Disney, but because it came with zero-percent interest and my dad used it to buy a new canoe. That's a joint account. Does she have one in her own name?

More important, does she know what she's doing? I mean, it's not like there's a bookstore in a fifty-mile radius where my mom can buy a guide to leaving your ex-cop husband and not have everyone in Scottsfield find out about it, including my dad. Scottsfield is about as far out in the sticks as you can be, which means that everyone knows everything about everyone except the things that really matter. Maybe Mom used the Internet at work. I try to be optimistic.

I go over to my desk and grab my photo album. I open to the first page. There we are: me, Mom, Dad, and Matt in front of the Statue of Liberty. Even Dad is smiling. I close the album and stick it in my bag.

Toothbrush! I knew I was forgetting something. I almost have it in my bag when I remember that I still need it for tonight.

And tomorrow morning. Why are we waiting for tomorrow? We should be leaving now. How are we going to make it through dinner with Dad?

A car door slams. He's home. My hands shake like I'm playing a solo during a band concert. I fumble with my tennis shoes, stuffing them into the bag, then I zip it and toss it onto the floor. I try to push it under the bed, but it's too tall. It keeps getting stuck.

Keys clink against the kitchen counter. I take the tennis shoes out of the bag, and yank at the zipper. It catches on a pair of shorts. *Forget about closing it.* I kick the bag under my bed.

"Hello? Where is everyone?" My dad's footsteps thump closer.

Is my mom's bag packed and stashed under the bed or does she have stuff strewn all over the room? I have to go with the stuff-strewn-everywhere version. Ever since Matt died, my mom doesn't do neat and tidy. She does chaos, which I guess is simply a reflection of how we all feel. Unfortunately it also means that I have to pick up the slack with cleaning. My dad requires counters to be dish free, coffee tables to be magazine free, and the laundry-room floor to be clothes free. That's just for starters.

I take my tennis shoes into the hall and plop myself in front of my dad to put them on. "Hi, Dad!"

"Hi, yourself. How was your day?" He speaks so normally, so rationally, some of the time.

"Great," I say. My voice comes out too high-pitched even for a girl. "I'm going biking. Want to come?"

Wrong question. He frowns and wanders off toward the window without responding. My dad hasn't been on a bike since Matt died. We used to go biking together all the time. Me, Matt, and Dad. Dad can't go running with us anymore because of the gunshot wound he got when he was a cop, but he can still bike. Funny thing is, when I bike I can still feel Matt riding next to me, hear the crunch of his wheels on the gravel. It's my dad who seems to be missing.

I finish tying my shoes and stand up. "I better ask Mom how long before dinner," I say, sprinting off toward my parents' bedroom.

My mom is busy straightening their comforter. The whole suitcase-under-the-bed thing has me nervously twirling my ponytail. It feels like a plane has crashed and the black box is beeping a signal at a frequency only I can hear. And I hope Dad never hears.

"I was just checking to see how long I had before dinner," I say from the doorway. Mom and I avoid looking at each other. It's easier that way. "I wanted to go for a bike ride."

"Sure, have fun," she says, a bit too loudly. "Be back in an hour."

I pedal down the dirt driveway, surrounded by twenty acres of hay and sweet smells. We don't farm—those acres are just a cushion between us and the rest of the world. Grasshoppers bounce along in front of my bike, trying to get out of the way. I look back at our house—white vinyl siding, black trim, and a green roof. There are lots of shrubs, stone frogs, gnomes, and fake dragonflies on metal stakes, but no more flowers. Gardening used to be my mom's hobby. We spent every Saturday one spring ripping out grass to make more flower beds, but this year Mom let the grass grow back in.

Chester, the neighbor's horse, is out in his field, tossing his head over the fence. Most afternoons I feed him carrots. My heart

skips. Will Chester be okay once I leave? Mr. Jenkins takes about
as much care of that horse as he does his house. In other words, not
much at all. His roof needs to be reshingled, the barn repainted, the
bushes trimmed, the fence repaired, the siding replaced. My dad has
a mental list of about a hundred things he thinks Jenkins needs to
do. Half the items most people could have come up with. The rest
are things only my dad would notice.

As I pedal, I think about my favorite TV show, *In Plain Sight*.
It's about the Witness Protection Program. I always thought it
would be exciting to hide behind a new identity. I just didn't
think it would actually happen to me. Also, I underestimated
the ache I would feel over never seeing my dad again. My dad
hasn't always been like this. Back when we lived in Philadelphia
and he was a cop, he was always smiling. After we moved to
Michigan, he smiled a lot less. Since my brother killed himself,
he's stopped smiling altogether. And he takes it out on my mom.
Me, he leaves alone.

My dad's voice echoes in my head. *What Matt did is your fault.*
What was I thinking? What if Dad's already figured out that we're
planning on leaving? What will he do to Mom? I shouldn't have left
her alone with him. Not that I'll be much help. I spin around and
bike home as fast as I can.

When I get back, the house smells of garlic mixed with oregano.
Spaghetti. My dad's favorite. How fitting for our last night together.
From the doorway I can hear the thud of silverware being laid down
on the table and the clink of glasses being carried together. Dad's

news program murmurs on the TV in the living room. He doesn't suspect. At least, not yet.

"I'm going to take a shower," I say. Not that anyone's listening.

The water trickles down my face. I love long, hot showers, but I only dare to take them when my dad's not home to scream at me for wasting water. Of course, he's never actually yelled at me about the water, just at Matt.

When we leave, I'm going to miss Zach most of all. I can't tell him what I'm going to be doing at lunchtime tomorrow. Not that I even really know myself. Still, I don't want him knowing anything that my dad can punch out of him.

Zach was a favorite topic of conversation for my therapist, Maureen. She had just graduated from shrink school, and I could tell she was a real fan of Freud. Which wasn't bad, since it meant she had a couch. Our first appointment went something like this:

"Who would you say your friends are?" she asked.

I kicked my shoes off and lay down on the couch. I liked the feel of the leather through my socks. I folded my hands under my neck and stared up at her ceiling.

"Zach."

She looked down at her notes. "Last week you said that he was your brother's best friend."

"Yeah, so?" I could see her trying to figure out which shrink theory that proved.

"How about girlfriends?"

I didn't want to talk about it. "No, Zach's not dating anyone at the moment."

"I mean, do you have any close friends who are girls?"

"Zach's my best friend. Lauren used to be my best friend, but we kind of lost touch after Matt died."

"And why is that?"

"Because of what I was doing the day Matt died."

"Which was?" She tilted her head, ready for me to tell all.

I glanced at her desk. "Nice flowers. Are they from your husband?"

Maureen nodded. My dad never gets flowers for my mom anymore. Probably just as well. She wouldn't notice them anyway.

Maureen never seemed annoyed when I didn't answer her questions. She just tried a new approach. "So it's basically just you and Zach now?"

"Yep."

"How does that make you feel?"

I went back to staring at the ceiling. "I don't know. Happy, I guess."

"Happy?"

"Sure. Zach acts a lot like my brother did. So sometimes I forget they're not the same person." I sat up and brushed my hands together. "Okay. Are we done here?"

The day after that, my dad smashed the Statue of Liberty. He made my mom call and tell Maureen I wouldn't be in to see her anymore. He said therapy is a waste of money. He also told her to upgrade the cable service and to order him a subscription to Military History *magazine. Then he went and bought a new fishing pole for Matt, who is dead.*

* * *

"Where's Matt? He's always late for dinner."

My dad often talks like he thinks Matt is still alive. To be fair, I do my share of pretending Matt's alive. But I don't vocalize it, at least, not most of the time.

I look down so my mom will answer. My wet hair brushes against the back of my neck, giving me a chill.

"I think he has a tutoring session with his history teacher. More cheesy bread, Ray?" She passes him the bread basket, then turns to me. "So how was school today?"

"Fine, I guess. Rachel spilled hydrochloric acid on herself in chem and had to use the emergency shower."

"She's okay, I hope," says Mom.

"Yeah, she's fine."

I look over at my dad. As usual, he's staring out at the fields, muttering to himself. The only word I catch is "oil." Although I know I should hate him, my heart tells me to talk to him since I may never see him again. My stupid, stupid heart.

I clear my throat. "So, Dad. How was work today?"

No answer.

"Dad," I say, a little louder. "How was work today?"

"Oil. Matt needs to change the oil in his car. How does he expect it to run if he doesn't change the oil?" He bangs his fist on the table for emphasis.

"Right. I'll remind him when he gets home," my mom cuts in. Then, in a fake-cheery voice that most people reserve for two-year-olds, she says, "Call volume was up today." It's her way of pretending that this conversation is perfectly normal. She makes a point of looking at both me and my dad when she talks, even though I'm the only one listening.

"That's great," I say. "Any special reason?"

"We were running a special on the Autumn Splendor sets. I showed you one of the plates, right?"

"Yeah, really cute."

Mom works in management for Essence dinnerware. She's always coming home with some sample or damaged merchandise. She loves all of those patterned plates and bowls—and especially the matching doodads that go with the sets, like place mats and candleholders. They even make piggy banks and snow globes. Mom has it all.

After dinner, Dad retreats to the basement and his trains. When he's in his muttering phase, he's usually pretty safe, so I follow. Dad's never actually hurt me, anyhow. He's just hurt Matt and my mom. Now just Mom. I'm not sure why, but I think the reason he leaves me alone has something to do with the trains. I am the one who comes down here with him, who watches him build and play. I am the one who goes with him on train-picture-taking missions. Together we have taken hundreds of pictures of trains. Maybe he thinks I understand him, get him.

I don't.

But I do the best job pretending.

Dad sits on a high gray swivel chair. I duck under the table and stand in the center cut-out. He flips a few switches and a steam engine emerges from an old brick engine house. It looks dusty, but only because he painted it that way.

Trains have a way of helping Dad talk coherently. "I thought I'd make the haunted house next," he says. Engines, boxcars, and building kits are all we get my dad for Christmas. Matt and I gave him the haunted house years ago, but he never put it together. His town has a grocery store, grain elevator, and an orange and green house Matt and I called the "pumpkin house." Soon it will have our haunted house. Too bad neither Matt nor I will be there to see it.

"You can put it right here," I say, pointing to an empty spot next to a cabin on the bank of the fake river. Dad designed the cabin to make it look like Ramona's Retreat, this place we used to go on vacation. It also has these little people standing around outside it, like the four of us.

"Too close."

"Good point," I say, nodding. In real life, the cabins near Ramona's Retreat are so far apart you can forget there are other people around. "How about next to the hardware store?"

"Sure. That sounds good." He smiles for the first time in a long while.

I stand and watch the trains travel around me, breathing in deeply the wet-potato basement smell that I love, but everyone else hates. And in this way, I say good-bye to Dad.

When I go back upstairs, Mom is watching our favorite soap, *The Winds of Change.* Mom let me start watching it with her when I was nine. I've been hooked ever since. It's on late enough in the afternoons that, if I want, I can watch it live after school, but usually I just wait and watch it on the DVR with Mom.

"Sorry I started without you," Mom says, hitting pause on the remote. "You want me to rewind?" She looks so pale and uncomfortable that I worry when Dad comes back up he's going to figure out what we're planning.

"No, it's okay." I sit down next to her. "You've got to try harder to look normal," I whisper.

She nods and takes a deep breath.

"What's happened with Julia?" I ask.

"She doesn't remember getting hit by the car. Or that Ramón isn't really her husband." Mom takes a handful of Ritz Bits and offers me the box.

"She doesn't remember that Ramón's her stalker? No way. What about the apartment? How did he explain why they don't have any pictures?" I pop a couple of crackers in my mouth.

"He said there'd been a fire." She shakes her head.

"Hmm. I guess that would explain why they don't have much furniture, either."

I wonder if that's what we'll say too, when we get to where we're going with just our duffel bags.

CHAPTER 2

Tuesday

Second period. Gym. God. I hope my new school doesn't have a PE requirement. I loathe all forms of organized sports. Why didn't we just leave last night? Or this morning? The gym smells like chalk, which I guess is better than sweat, but not by much. I try not to breathe in too deeply.

Today is volleyball. I especially hate the bump hit. It's just wrong to hit a ball with that part of your arms. If I can't hit it with my hands, I'm not hitting the damn thing at all.

The ball is heading straight toward me. Great. Then I think of my dad kicking my mom and this time I slam it across the net. No one expects anything more than a wimpy hit. Most of the girls, in fact, see the ball heading for me and start up conversations, moving out of position. Including Jessica Hamilton. She gets hit smack in the nose. It starts to bleed.

"Who did that?"

"Was that Sara?"

I confirm my guilt by running over to Jessica and offering her a crumpled tissue from my pocket. "I'm really sorry, Jessica."

She grunts back. I can't tell if that's a "you're forgiven" grunt or an "I hate your guts" grunt. I hope it isn't the latter. I hate having people mad at me.

We take a five-minute break while Mrs. Koster takes Jessica and Stephanie to the nurse. Jessica for her nose, and Stephanie because she fainted at the sight of Jessica's blood. Blood doesn't bother me. I'm used to it. Unfortunately, once Mrs. Koster gets back, she makes us keep playing.

The opposing team usually hits the ball to me, since most days I deliberately miss. So even after my nose-busting, blood-squirting return, the girls, in their forgetful laziness, continue to send the ball toward me. In my freaked-out frenzy I fire them all back, racking up points for my team, and we win by sixteen points.

"Hey, Sara, good game," says Jamie. "You should come out for the team." If I were staying, I could just imagine the next gym class. I would be first pick; the captain would be psyched. Cue replay of the third-grade kickball game the day after I caught three fly balls in a row. It was a disaster. I disappointed everyone, especially myself. Short version: On a normal day, I suck.

English is on the third floor in the old part of the building. I love having classes there. It's like going back in time. When they installed whiteboards in the rest of the building, they skipped the six rooms on the third floor. You would think it was because they ran out of money, but I'm betting the truth is that Mrs. Monroe refused to part with her blackboard. Mrs. Monroe is way into chalk.

The wooden floors creak as all the students come in and take their seats. Mrs. Monroe's clunky heels make soft thuds as she walks across the room and opens the wall of windows to let in the breeze. Mrs. Monroe likes to pretend that she's mean. I had her last year too, and she even dressed up as a witch for Halloween because she said it was a reflection of her personality. Then she gave us chocolate and no homework.

Our free writing topic is on the blackboard. We always spend the first ten minutes of English class doing a free writing assignment. This usually stresses me out because I can't write fast. I agonize over every word, even though I know it's graded only on completeness and Mrs. Monroe is the only one who'll read it.

Today the topic is "A Person I Admire." I don't know if it's the topic or the fact that I know I'm never coming back, but I let it all out. As the idea comes to me, I feel a tingling in my toes. I start right away, before the bell rings. Maybe that's cheating since we're only supposed to write for ten minutes, but for once I don't want to wait.

The person I most admire is my big brother, Matt. He killed himself, but that's not why I admire him. I'm mad at him for that. But I've pretty much forgiven him for any other faults he had, which weren't many.

Matt and I were a year and a half apart. When we were little, we were inseparable. We played with nearly everything together: LEGOs and grocery carts, Hot Wheels and Play-Doh, army guys and jump ropes.

As we grew older, Matt and I turned out to be about as opposite as you can get: I got As; Matt mainly Cs (except in Spanish; that was an A). When Dad told me to do something, I did it right away. When Dad told Matt to do something, he only did it if he didn't have something better to do. Me: would rather go to the dentist than play sports. Matt: soccer fiend. At an amusement park, my idea of living dangerously is riding the Ferris Wheel; Matt wasn't happy unless he spent at least fifty percent of the time upside down. While we were opposites, it was a good kind of opposite and it never stopped us from being close.

The bell rings. I stop writing for a second. I haven't really said why I admired Matt. Then again, Mrs. Monroe always tells us that we don't have to rigidly keep to the topic; the important thing is to keep the pen moving. Still, I try to get to the admiration part.

*I wish I could play piano like Matt—
he was a natural.*

*Matt loved me. He hugged me. He
played with me. He picked me up when I
fell, both at five and at fifteen. He was
my big brother. I adored him.*

*Matt was always there for the
people who needed him. That's what I
admired most about him.*

*Somehow none of us were there for
him the day he needed us most.*

I put down my pen. I haven't filled the page and time isn't up, but I've said all I need to.

"Your projects need to be about a significant event in world history. You can work on your own or with a partner. I'm giving you two months. Whatever you do, don't wait until the last minute."

Everyone in my history class groans except for me. I'm not bothering to listen to or take notes on anything that isn't due today. Mr. Robertson drones on about academic integrity and properly citing sources.

"You should all be taking notes on this," Robertson says, frowning at me and a couple of other slackers. 11:40 a.m. In fifteen minutes I'll be out of here. Forever.

I get out a pencil and a piece of paper and write down a few lines so it looks like I'm paying attention. I write:

Don't listen to your heart.
Can't trust Dad.
Must not tell.

Then I slip *Cujo* (a Stephen King book) out of my backpack and open it on my lap. I keep the pencil in my hand so it looks like I'm taking notes. I start to read. History fades away as I get lost in the story. My stomach churns. I hold my breath, afraid of what will happen when I turn the page.

Bang!

I jump in my seat, nearly knocking my water bottle off my desk. My heart races. *The door! Who just came in?* I can't look. Is my dad coming to get me out of class? Has he figured out that we're leaving?

I crumple up the paper on my desk. *What do I do with it? Do I try to throw it out?*

No time. I stuff it in my backpack and pray Dad doesn't find it.

I imagine Dad explaining to Robertson that I need to be excused for a dentist appointment, then yanking my shirt collar and dragging me down the hallway. Does anyone actually monitor the security cameras?

"Hi there," Alex Maloy says, to no one and to everyone as he saunters to his seat. I've never been so happy to see anyone as I am to see Alex at that moment. I think I even smile at him. I definitely notice how hot he looks when he doesn't shave. Today he's wearing a Notre Dame football shirt. Most days he wears college football T-shirts. Not that I pay attention.

"Pass?" asks Mr. Robertson, out of simple reflex, I'm sure, since Alex never has one.

"Did I need one of those? Hold on—let me go get you one."

"Just sit down," says Robertson. *Good call.* Everyone knows that if Alex Maloy leaves the room he'll never be back. Alex hasn't always had attendance issues, but he's certainly making up for lost time. Last year Alex seemed like the rest of us—reasonably interested in turning in homework and passing classes. Now, none of that seems to matter to him, but not in a depressing way. No; Alex is relaxed, confident, and friendly to everyone. So you can't help but hope that it won't all come crashing down if he doesn't get into a good football college.

Alex sits in the only free seat, which happens to be next to mine.

"Whatcha reading?" he whispers as Robertson runs through a list of possible topics.

Oh my God. He's not actually talking to me, is he? My cheeks heat up and I know they've just turned three shades of scarlet. Trying to act casual, I show him the cover. He lifts his eyebrows and looks back and forth between the book and me. "I never would have guessed," he says. "Can I see it?"

I pass him the book.

Act natural, Sara. As if guys like Alex Maloy ask you questions every day.

I sneak my cell phone under my desk and check my text messages. There's one from Zach, asking what movie I want to see Sunday afternoon. We go to a matinee most Sundays. It's cheap and it gets me out of the house. I can either pretend I didn't get the message or that I'll be around on Sunday. There's no way I can tell Zach the truth. If he knows anything and my dad asks him about it—it will show in his eyes. Zach can't lie. And I know my dad will ask him when we don't come home tonight because although he's currently Robot Dad, he's a very cunning robot.

PICK WHEN GET THERE, I text. EAT LUNCH W/O ME.

A minute later I have Zach's reply. WHY??

I turn off the phone.

Alex hands me back the book. "Have you read *Misery*?" he whispers.

Now it's my turn to look surprised. Wow. I guess I need to readjust my football player stereotype. I glance over at Robertson and try to talk without moving my lips. "No—that's another Stephen King one, isn't it?"

"Yeah, I can loan it to you. I'm almost done."

As long as you finish it in the next ten minutes and you don't care that you'll never get it back, I think. "Sure, thanks" is what I say.

When the bell rings, I'm out of my seat and at the door. So is everyone else. I have this urge to push everyone out of the way, but instead I wait my turn like I always do. Then I take the stairs two at a time, run outside, and cross in the middle of the street without really looking. Traffic in Scottsfield is practically nonexistent. Scottsfield doesn't have any actual traffic lights, just this one blinking light at the intersection of Main and Scott Streets. It blinks yellow on Main (slow down, you might actually see another car) and red on Scott. All the businesses in Scottsfield—all eight of them—are on Main Street along a two-block stretch. We've lived in Scottsfield for six years, and it feels like I've lived here forever. Even before we moved from Philadelphia, we would come for a week in the summer and during Christmas vacation, because my grandparents (on my dad's side) used to live here.

I make my way to the Dairy Dream. Me and everyone else. We're all going there or to Lucy's, the only restaurant in Scottsfield. We have an open campus, which means that as long as you're back for afternoon classes, you can go where you want for lunch.

I walk by myself, eavesdropping on the conversations around me. Amber and Melanie are talking about Amber's roots. Melanie keeps insisting that they're barely noticeable. *Hello.* They're about as noticeable as a hippo in a flower garden. Cameron is laughing so hard he's staggering all over the sidewalk. *Breathe already.* Then there's Josh and Kevin, discussing some game on TV last night. Kevin says the word "shit" eight times. After that I stop counting. Finally, there's me. Surrounded by people yet completely alone, already missing Amber's roots and Kevin saying "shit" and everything about this lame-ass town.

I'm wearing jeans and a short-sleeve T-shirt and starting to feel kind of cold. Yesterday was so warm—what's up with today?

When I get to the Dairy Dream, I'm not sure what I should do. I'm too nervous to be hungry, which is a good thing since I didn't bring a lunch and the Dairy Dream only sells variations on ice cream, nothing actually nutritious.

For a while I sit on one of those yellow parking space markers, waiting for Mom, but then a car comes and some guy wants to park in my spot, even though there are plenty of other spaces. *Jerk.* So I stand up and head toward the outdoor counter, keeping my eyes on the street.

Something cold smashes into my chest. Alex Maloy's chocolate ice-cream cone.

"Shit." That's Alex. I'm thinking the same thing, but I hold it in.

"Sorry. Here, let me wipe that for you," Alex says, napkin poised.

He blushes as he realizes where the ice cream landed. "I mean, here you go. Here's a napkin."

He chucks the remnants of his cone into a garbage can as I wipe.

"Guess I'll get another one." He looks me in the eyes. "You want a cone, Sara?"

I get this fluttery feeling in my stomach.

"Okay," I say, even though I'm not hungry. I can stuff down an ice cream if it means spending a few more minutes with Alex.

I take a quick look around to see if my mom's pulled up while I wasn't paying attention.

"Oh, that's right, you're Zach's girl," he says, tapping his forehead.

"I'm not Zach's girl." I go with what I imagine to be a coy smile. "We're friends, that's all."

"Huh. Does that make you available, then?"

Oh God. I nearly faint.

"Just for the next ten minutes." *After that, you'll never see me again.*

I can tell that he doesn't know how to take that. He laughs. "Chocolate or vanilla?"

"Vanilla, please," I say. I'm too wired to notice what I'm eating anyhow. I give my ponytail a nervous twirl.

"Two vanilla cones, please," Alex says to Jessica's mom, who's working the lunch shift. Mrs. Hamilton was a stay-at-home mom up until last spring. I'm pretty sure the only reason she took the job is so she can keep tabs on her daughter. Jessica never goes to the Dairy Dream anymore. But Mrs. Hamilton still loves the job because she's able to pump us for information about her.

"Hi, Sara, nice to see you," Mrs. Hamilton says as she hands me my cone. "Have you seen Jessica today? She seemed a little down this morning."

She seemed fine to me until I hit her in the nose with a volley-ball. Amazingly no one has mentioned that to Mrs. Hamilton yet. Apparently I still have friends, even though I haven't been all that social lately. "Yeah, she *did* look kind of depressed." Maybe Mrs. Hamilton will think she got the puffy nose from crying.

"See, you noticed it too. Glad to know I'm not just imagining things."

Mrs. Hamilton hands us our cones. I move away quickly before she can ask any more questions.

I scan the parking lot. *Where's my mom? Did something go wrong?*

"So what is it we have to do for the history paper?" Alex asks, licking his cone.

Here I am, on the verge of totally and completely freaking out about my mom, and Alex is asking me about a history paper. I want to tell him everything right then and there. But, let's face it: Besides the whole *Cujo* thing, Alex is basically a stranger. A dark-haired, drop-dead gorgeous stranger, but a stranger nonetheless. So instead I say, "No idea."

"Yeah, right."

"Seriously, no idea. I wasn't paying any attention and I didn't take a single note." I notice a streak of ice cream on his chin and point at my own chin as a hint.

He doesn't get it. He just scrunches his eyebrows and says, "Hey, that's my kind of girl. High five!"

I slap his hand back. Mine feels kind of tingly afterward.

"Hey, Alex!" shouts Jared from the sidewalk. "Ready to head back?"

"Go on ahead," he says, waving. "Catch you later." He winks at me. "Why don't we sit at a picnic table?"

I shrug, as if I haven't been dying for him to suggest it.

Alex sits down, facing the street. I sit next to him so I can watch the street too. He probably thinks I'm coming on to him. Maybe I am. Where *is* my mom?

"How about algebra for this afternoon. Can I copy yours?"

"Didn't do it." He still has that smudge on his chin. Can't he feel it?

He looks at me suspiciously. "You always do your homework. You just don't want me to copy."

"Not last night." You don't do homework when you know you won't be in class.

"So which do you like better, geometry or algebra?"

It isn't the sort of question I expect from Alex. I look around to see if there are any teachers he's trying to impress. Not a one. "Algebra, definitely."

"Why?"

"If you follow the rules, you get the right answers."

"Not me, man. If they had geometry two instead of algebra two, I'd be acing it."

I raise one eyebrow.

"What? You think I'm not capable of good grades?" he says, a touch defensively.

"Are you?"

"If I like the subject, I am. Gotta love those geometric proofs."

I make a face. "I hate proofs. They're too much like the puzzles my dad always makes us do while we're on vacation."

"So where do you go on vacation that you have time for puzzles?" Alex crumples his napkin into a ball and tosses it from hand to hand.

"We used to rent this cabin—Ramona's Retreat—about an hour away on the Au Sable River. Way out in the middle of nowhere. Even more in the middle of nowhere than here. One of those places where there's no street signs, just a bunch of markers with arrows pointing the way to various cabins."

"You're kidding—my folks own a cabin near there. I remember the signs for it. The name kind of sticks out. Our sign just has our last name on it."

"Yeah, yours and pretty much everyone else's."

Alex drops his napkin ball under the table and bends to retrieve it. A silver car approaches. I hold my breath.

Not Mom's car. I let my breath back out and check my watch. What does "lunch" *mean*? Does my mom have any clue as to when my lunch is? Suppose she already came before I got here. She'd come back, wouldn't she?

I pull out my cell and dial my mom.

"Who are you calling?" asks Alex.

I ignore him.

The call goes straight to voice mail. Figures. My mom doesn't completely embrace technology and almost never turns on her phone except when she's making a call. I put the phone back in my pocket and check my watch again.

"You seem worried about the time," Alex says. "You want to head back?"

I shake my head. He still has that blob of ice cream on his chin.

"It's only ten minutes before fifth period. You're not planning on skipping, are you?"

Alex must see the "I'm about to puke" look on my face, because he stops grinning, leans in closer, and asks, "Is something wrong?"

I shake my head and try to smile so he'll get up and leave. What I really want to do is hold on to his hand and make him stay here so I won't be alone.

And because I like him.

"No, everything's fine. I just don't feel like going back yet."

"Well, okay then. I guess I'll be the good student for once." Alex gets up and stands there awkwardly a few moments.

I hand him a napkin. "You've got ice cream on your chin."

He wipes it off, stuffs the napkin in his pocket, and starts walking. "Don't worry," he says, looking back over his shoulder. "I won't say anything."

The wind starts to blow. We really should have had hot chocolate today, not ice cream. I wish I had worn a sweatshirt. At least there's one in my duffel bag, which should be here soon. Has to be here soon. I want to lay my head down because it's spinning, but I can't because I might miss seeing my mom's car.

Why isn't she here yet? Panic bumps around inside me, like I've swallowed a jack-in-the-box and can't get the lid closed again.

Mom, where are you?

CHAPTER 3

Tuesday

Pretty soon I'm the only one left at the Dairy Dream. All the high school students have gone back to class and the few adults who stopped by have returned to work. I can feel Mrs. Hamilton's eyes on my back. If I don't leave, I'm sure she'll call Altman. That's our superstrict assistant principal. She probably has him on speed dial; she's the type. I stand up and head in the direction of school, scanning for Mom's car.

The problem with a town the size of Scottsfield is that there are no crowds to get lost in and no shops to even browse. Unless you count the Feed-and-Seed, which is where I stop. They have a display in front of the store. I pause to look at the salt licks. Sometimes we buy them for the deer that hang out in our field.

"Sara?"

I turn around. It's Jack Reynolds. He stands so close I can smell his sewer breath. Jack and my dad both graduated from Scottsfield High the same year. They were best buddies. Still are. Jack is a cop, like my dad used to be when we lived in Philadelphia.

"Hi." I try to sound nonchalant, but I can hear the quiver in my voice. I clear my throat. "How are you?"

"Fine, just fine. How are you all holding up? It's been four months now since—"

Tact has always eluded Jack. "Yeah, about that," I say. "We're fine. Just fine." If he believes that, he's a moron.

"Shouldn't you be in school now?"

I examine my watch—a scratched-up old Timex with a sun and moon that rotates as time passes. No need to read the time; I already have that memorized from when I checked a minute ago. "You're right. I was at the Dairy Dream for lunch and I must've lost track of time. I better get back."

"Guess you better. Be seeing you, then." Jack runs his fingers through his greasy hair.

Neither of us moves. I pretend to check out the price of the salt licks.

"You shouldn't put those out for deer, you know," he says. "Some folks will hunt them that way. Takes all the sport out of it, in my opinion."

What an idiot. As if we even keep guns in the house anymore.

Ignoring him, I walk away.

"Sara?"

I turn around and sweep my eyes across the Dairy Dream parking lot as I wait for him to speak.

"Say hi to your dad for me."

I freeze. Jack is grinning like a wolf.

The day after my dad smashed the Statue of Liberty, my mom and I went to the Scottsfield police station to file a report. Jack took my mom's statement, only he didn't write anything down. He said, "I've known Ray a long time. He's a good man. It takes a lot out of a man to see his son go that way. Give him some space. A little understanding. I'm sure things will work themselves out." Then he gave Mom a pat on the shoulder and sent us home.

When Dad came home that night, we knew that Jack had called him. Dad stomped in, slamming the door. Mom's hand jerked away from the wooden spoon she was using to stir the ground beef. I stopped drying the glass in my hands and clutched it to me like a baby.

"What lies have you been telling Jack about me, Michelle?"

"I just ... I thought ..."

Dad's face was red, his eyes narrow. "You thought what? That you wanted me in jail? Is that what you thought? Do you know what they do to cops in jail?" Dad skipped over the fact that he's no longer a cop.

"No, I ... Of course I ..." She stepped away from the stove to get further away from my dad. Big mistake.

My dad whipped the towel off the counter and pulled the cast-iron pan from the front burner. Then he flung it at my mom. Ground beef flew in all directions as the heavy pan hit her foot with a *thunk*. She was still wearing dress shoes and nylons. The nylons melted and stuck to her foot. I can still hear her scream when I close my eyes. Once again I did nothing, said nothing, changed nothing. What kind of daughter was I?

At the hospital she said it was an accident. She dropped the pan on her own foot. After that she stayed away from Jack Reynolds.

And now that same man is staring at me with his wolf eyes. "Okay," I say.

I turn and walk away quickly, hoping his walkie-talkie will crackle to life with news of a crime or car accident to distract him. I know the odds aren't in my favor. Nothing ever happens in Scottsfield. Except to my family, that is.

I force myself to count to a hundred before I look over my shoulder. Jack is still watching me. Why the hell can't he leave me alone? I cross at the blinking light in front of the school and then dare to look back. He seems to be gone. I run as fast as I can back to the Dairy Dream.

I pull my phone out and try my mom's cell again. I call her work number, but it goes straight to voice mail. Then I try our home phone. Nothing.

Next to the Dairy Dream is Dr. Duncan's office. He's the town dentist. We don't go to him. I've heard he's a hack. I can't very well sit in the waiting room all afternoon for an appointment that I don't have, or ask for a consultation and end up with a filling I don't need. Since the parking lot is in the front of the building, I decide to hide out in the back. I still have a good view.

Pressing my back against the building, I turn my face so I can watch the Dairy Dream. I stay like that for about a half hour, until I'm sick of standing.

I try crouching down but that's too much trouble, so finally I just sit on the grass. Which isn't the greatest idea, because now it's raining. The only way I could stay dry under the overhang would be if I were a superskinny person like Melanie Rogers. Don't get me wrong, I'm not fat—but only thanks to my hyperactive metabolism and not my willpower. Big drips keep streaming off the edge of the overhang and landing in the middle of my hair.

I'm cold, tired, and wet, and I'm also freaking out. It's past three o'clock and still there's no sign of my mom. At least school is out, so I no longer have to hide behind a dentist's office. I get up and walk like Frankenstein to keep my damp jeans from rubbing too much against my legs.

The Scottsfield Public Library is on the other side of the Dairy Dream. As I walk into the tiny building, the head librarian, Mrs. Evans, looks up and frowns at me. I wish the other librarian, Mrs. Scott (Scottsfield is named after her family), was here. Mrs. Scott always greets me by name and asks how she can help. Mrs. Evans is about twenty years past a normal retirement and seems to deliberately not recognize me, even though I'm what anyone would consider to be a regular. I'm glad I didn't try to hide out there while school was in session. She would have called the school on me within minutes.

The library is made up of a single small room sectioned off by a bunch of strangely painted bookshelves. I sit down at a table in the children's section because it's directly in front of the big picture window.

"What are you doing here?" says a little voice. "This is the kids' section."

"Billy!" His mom, Mrs. Harper, gives me an apologetic look. She's a sweet lady who owns a riding stable over in Brookton, where you can rent horses by the hour. Matt and I used to go there sometimes. She always fed us cookies after we'd ridden.

"Don't worry about it," I say to Mrs. Harper. I try to feel flattered that I've just been referred to as an adult. Even if it was by a five-year-old. "I'm watching for my mom." It's refreshing to actually tell the truth.

"Oh. You want to read me a book?" Billy holds up a big book with a dinosaur on the front cover. Matt was obsessed with dinosaurs too at that age.

"Billy, I'm sure she's busy."

"Actually I would, but I don't want to miss seeing my mom. She'll be in a hurry to pick me up." Billy looks so disappointed that I wish I could change my mind.

Billy and his mom leave, and the library is empty for a while. Mrs. Evans rearranges the books displayed in the window. I get the urge to shout "Get out of my way! I can't see!" but I don't want her calling the cops (i.e., Jack Reynolds) to throw me out of the place, so I keep my mouth shut.

Mrs. Evans comes over to the table and makes a big production of reaching around me to put away books that have been strewn all over. She sighs as if I'm responsible for the mess. Some kid left a drawing on the table. Mrs. Evans picks it up. With a disgusted frown, she crumples it and throws it away. I think back to another piece of paper destined for the trash. It came in the mail addressed to Matt. A pamphlet from Middlebury College. Think Vermont.

Snow. Peaceful. Especially peaceful. My dad had it poised over the garbage can as he was sorting the mail, but Matt plucked it away at the last second.

"Hey, wait," he said. "I've heard of this place. They specialize in languages. You're assigned to dorms based on the language you're studying and you have to sign a pact that you'll only speak in that language." Matt was a whiz at languages. Mrs. Jameson said that Matt was the best Spanish student she'd had in years. Spanish is the only foreign language you can take in Scottsfield, but Matt didn't let that stop him. He borrowed Teach Yourself Chinese CDs from the library and listened to them at home for fun.

"You don't need to learn a foreign language to live in Scottsfield," said Dad. "Everyone speaks English here. Besides, we don't have the money for a fancy private college. Brookton Community College will do just fine. You can live at home and work at the hardware store on weekends to pay for it. End of story." Dad snatched the flyer from Matt's hand, ripped it in half, and stuffed it in the trash.

Matt reached defiantly into the garbage can and pulled it back out. Then Dad punched Matt in the face.

When people asked, Matt said he got the black eye playing baseball with his sister. Which fit really well, since everyone knows I'm terrible at sports. It didn't of course explain why I would have agreed to play baseball with him in the first place, but most people didn't make that connection. Just Zach.

At five minutes before seven, Mrs. Evans flicks the lights, even though I'm the only person there. I stay where I am. At seven o'clock, she turns them out completely. I use the bit of light coming through the picture window to find my way out of the building. Mrs. Evans locks the door behind us and takes off down the street without even a glance at me or a good-bye. It's only drizzling now, and I'm somewhat dried out from the library, but I'm still miserable from the cold and from how I'm feeling inside.

In front of the library there's a red bench next to a planter of flowers. I lay my backpack on the bench and sit on top of it, vaguely hoping it'll keep the water on the bench from soaking through my pants. I slope forward a little because my history binder is still in my backpack from before lunch. Which, come to think of it, I never ate. Unless you count the ice-cream cone. Which I don't. I like to eat, most of the time.

It's better to think of food than what must have happened to my mom. So I try to think of what I'd eat if I could just imagine something and it would appear right in front of me. Only, I think of spaghetti. Which brings me back to last night. And my dad. Surely Mom isn't at home fixing supper for him, our plan forgotten. Is she?

A silver car speeds past going at least forty in a twenty-five. Not my mom's. But it puts on its brakes a little way down the street and does a U-turn. The car slows as it approaches my bench, and the window comes down.

"Sara?"

"Hi, Alex."

"What are you still doing downtown?" Alex asks.

I shrug my shoulders.

"Have you eaten dinner?"

I shake my head.

"Hop in. I'll treat you to a burger at Lucy's."

"I'm kind of waiting for someone."

"I don't mean to pry or anything, but it seems like you've been waiting for this person all day. I don't think they're going to show up. Have you tried calling?"

I nod, blinking hard to keep from crying.

"Look, I'm sorry. Are you sure you don't want to get something to eat?"

I take one last look down the road, then I open the passenger door and get in. Well, I try to get in. First I have to wait for Alex to clear the fast-food wrappers off the front seat.

"You must drive around a lot," I say, mainly to avoid thinking and talking about my mom. We don't have any fast-food restaurants in Scottsfield.

Alex looks a little sheepish. "Not really, actually. It's just that I don't clean my car out very often."

Alex does another illegal U-turn and drives the half block to Lucy's.

"Let's sit here," I say, pointing to a booth in front of the window. At least I can still watch for my mom, although it's starting to get darker and harder to see.

Lacey (Lucy's sister) is our waitress. "What can I get for you today?" she asks. She's so cheery, I want to vomit. My life is spinning out of control—for her, probably the worst thing that's going to happen is that she'll mix up a hamburger order.

While I concentrate on an approaching set of headlights, Alex orders. "I'll have a cheeseburger with fries and a Coke."

"I'll have the same, except make mine a root beer," I say, still tracking the headlights. Matt and I used to drink root beer all the time when we were little. I'd stopped drinking it at about age ten. It's too sweet. I took it up again after Matt died because whenever I take the first sip I get this *whoosh* feeling and I think—just for a second—that I'm sitting on the porch swing next to Matt.

"You missed a thrilling algebra lesson," Alex says. "Something about *x* and *y*, I think."

I'm having a hard time focusing on what he's saying.

"Okay, so that wasn't very funny." He clears his throat. "There's a party Saturday night at Nick Russell's house. Want to go?"

"Why?" I ask absently.

Alex looks confused.

"You mean why did I ask you to the party?"

I nod.

"I don't know—you seem kind of depressed. I thought it might cheer you up." He pauses. "That, and I can't think of anything else to say."

I laugh a tiny bit.

Alex gets a happy smile on his face.

Lacey brings us the cheeseburgers, but she forgot the cheese on mine. I eat it anyway. What does it matter?

"So you want to go see a movie or something?" Alex asks.

My heart thumps. "Now?"

"Why not?"

I say what's easiest and what Alex would expect from me: "It's a school night."

"See, I knew you were a straight shooter. That skipping-algebra thing was just a fluke, wasn't it?" He showers his fries with salt and then points the shaker at me. "In fact, you probably only skipped because you hadn't done the homework. No. That can't be it. You didn't do the homework because you knew you weren't going to class. Am I right?"

I want to answer because he's so cute and sweet, but I can't.

Tell no one.

Alex clears his throat. "So are you coming to the football game Friday night?"

"Unfortunately, yes. I hate football, but I play in the band." And, in my head, I'm really hoping I won't be here on Friday.

"Okay then," says Alex, as if I've just insulted him.

I realize my stupidity. "Oh, right, sorry." Alex is on the football team. "I'm sure you'll do a great job."

The darker it gets, the more worried I feel. I finish my burger and fries in record time. Alex is only about halfway through his when I get up. "Can you take me home, please?" I say, digging through my purse for some money.

"Let me just get a box and the check," he says. "My treat."

An electric charge surges through my body. All of a sudden I feel like we're on a date. Me and Alex Maloy? Matt would have laughed his head off.

We cruise down Scottsfield Highway going at least seventy in a fifty-five. When I apply the imaginary brake on my side of the car, my foot crunches down on a CD case. I pick it up. "You have a *Smooth Seventies* CD?"

"My mom's," he says. "She had to borrow my car last week while hers was in the shop."

"Does it have 'Wildfire' on it?"

"Try it and see."

I slip it into the player and skip through the tracks until I get to the one I'm looking for. My mom used to play "Wildfire" on the stereo all the time. It's the song I was trying to play the day Dad snapped. The song has something to do with a horse and a woman who's chasing after it in a blizzard. That's all I really remember, since each time I listen to it I get caught up in the chorus and forget to pay attention to how the story comes out. With the speakers blaring and Alex and I flying down the road, I kind of feel like I'm on the back of that runaway horse.

The song ends and I turn off the stereo. I've managed to space out again, so I still don't know how it turns out. Did she find the horse or not?

I check out Alex's profile. He seems mellow, relaxed, without a care in the world. Although we're going fast, I feel safe. Protected. I almost tell him about my mom, but I want him to stay like he is.

It starts to rain harder. We ride in a silence that might have been uncomfortable if this were a date, but since I'm trying to pretend it isn't, I simply lean my head back against the headrest and think about the rain and my mom, and pretty soon I'm back at my eleventh birthday party.

* * *

"Girl!"

"Umbrella!"

"Rain!"

"American Idol!"

"Singing in the rain!"

"You got it!" My mom pointed at Amber. "Your turn." Amber got up and took the dry erase marker from my mom. She twirled it in her fingers for a few seconds, then started to draw.

"Your mom is so cool," Lauren said. We were sitting next to each other cross-legged on the floor.

I shrugged. At all of the other parties I'd ever been to, there was an unspoken agreement that moms were to keep their distance. My mom was the only mom who dared to hang out with us. Of course, the only reason that my mom was so fun and happy was because my dad was away for the weekend. Which was the only reason I was allowed to have the party in the first place.

Alex taps his fingers on the steering wheel, dragging me back into the present. "That your house?"

"Yeah, this is it." Fear crawls up my legs.

"It's awfully dark. Don't you guys believe in lights?"

"A waste of electricity," I say weakly.

"Your parents out?"

"Looks like it," I say.

"Want me to come in and wait with you?" From the way he says it, I get the feeling that he has more in mind than just waiting.

That would be great, except my dad hates when I have friends over.
Even if you were to leave the second he got home, he'd still be mad.

"Nah. I'll just light a few candles. Read a little Stephen King.
It'll be great."

Alex laughs and puts the car in park.

Should I really go in? Maybe I should just ask him to drive me
back to the Dairy Dream. I open the car door and the dome light
illuminates Alex's face. Is this the last time I'll see him? My brain
divides itself into two teams, one that's cheering for the answer to
be yes, and the other for no. I imagine myself in his backseat, making out with him, his hands in my hair. My tongue in his mouth.
I feel myself blush and realize that I've been staring. Only, I think
he's been staring too. He gets this funny look on his face and starts
leaning in closer to me. I chicken out at the last second and turn
my head.

"Guess I should go in," I say. *Idiot! You just blew your last chance*
to kiss those lips! What were you thinking?

"I suppose so," says Alex. "Bye, then."

"Bye. Thanks for the ride."

I wave and walk up the front porch. All thoughts of kissing
Alex, of happiness, of anything good, disappear as I touch the cool
door handle. What's on the other side of the door? I feel like I'm in
the oatmeal dream again. Sick. Drowning.

There's no smell of dinner, no one reading in the living room.
The house feels empty. I walk into the kitchen and turn on a light.
There are no pots on the stove, no dishes in the sink. I continue to
the living room and have this urge to turn the TV on so the house

will stop being so quiet. My heart pounding, I make my way down the hallway to my parents' room and turn on the light.

I stifle a scream. My dad is sitting on the bed, fully clothed, completely awake. In the dark.

"I didn't think anyone was home," I say.

My dad just stares. I'm used to his silences by now, but this is excruciating.

"Your mom's gone," he says matter-of-factly.

It's like I'm trapped inside some Stephen King novel instead of my own life. How does Dad know? And why am I not with her?

"What?" I ask finally.

My dad reaches over to the nightstand and gets his pack of cigarettes. He shakes out the last one, lights it, and takes a drag, blowing the smoke up at the ceiling. He crumples the empty pack and tosses it at me. It bounces off my arm.

"Training seminar in North Carolina. The person who was supposed to go got food poisoning, so they sent your mom."

"When is she coming back?"

"A week or so."

My dad takes another puff of his cigarette, then flips on the TV and doesn't say another word—he just sits there and smokes. I want to wave my hands in front of his face and make him tell me more, but he would probably break my arm. So instead I back away.

The first thing I notice when I get to my room is that Sam, my stuffed dog, is on my bed. My back starts to feel prickly. I know I put Sam in my duffel bag. I look at my desk. My photo album sits neatly on the corner.

I go to my bathroom. My toothbrush is in its place in the yellow duck holder.

My whole body shakes. With an urge to scream, I pick up the edge of my comforter and peek under my bed. My duffel bag is there. But it's empty. Someone has put everything back where it belongs. But who?

I lie on the floor and hug my arms to my chest. I try to calm down by concentrating on breathing slower. In, out. In, out. *Mom, Dad.* In, out. *Mom, Dad. Mom, Dad. Mom, Dad.* It isn't working. The worry builds to a crescendo in my head.

I force myself to think, *MOM.* I say it in my head as loud as I can. *MOM.* It must have been *MOM* who put everything back. Even though everything has been put back very neatly and precisely, the way Dad would do it. For some reason Mom must have known she wouldn't be able to pick me up today, so she put everything back. *Hey, wait a minute—maybe she unpacked my bag and left a note!*

I sweep my arm under the bed and fish out my duffel bag. I tear the main zipper open and feel around all over the inside. Then I try the top zipper and both side ones. A scream grows from the tips of my toes and ripples through my entire body until I have to cover my mouth with my stuffed dog to keep it in.

Mom, Dad, Mom, Dad is turning into just *Dad, Dad, Dad. Dad* unpacked my bag. I shake my head, trying to come up with something that makes sense. If Dad thought he could drive me crazy, make me doubt what my mom and I planned, it's working.

If my dad put everything back, where's my mom?

Dad's voice echoes in my mind. *Don't even think of leaving.*

What if he caught her dragging my bag out to the car?

I will find you. Guaranteed.

I have to get out of here. I snatch my duffel off the floor and put it on my bed. I dump all the contents of my drawers onto the floor in massive piles, then I start flinging things into the bag at random. Pants, shorts, T-shirts, shoes, a handful of socks. I take my photo album and slam it down as hard as I can into the bag.

And then I lie down on the floor and cry. Because I know I can't leave. Maybe my dad came home while Mom was putting her suitcase in the car and she had to make up the story about the training seminar. Maybe she decided to change the plan, to find someplace for us to live first. If that's the case, she'll be coming back for me. And I have to be here when she does.

Even if it kills me.

CHAPTER 4

Wednesday

My alarm clock moos. It's one of those novelty kinds that's shaped like a cow. Matt bought it for me because he knew how much I hate things that beep.

I open my eyes and stare at the Picasso print on my wall. Picasso's my favorite artist. I like his stuff because of all the bright colors. That, and it's ugly. Take the *Portrait of Dora Maar*. She's this lady with, like, three quarters of a yellow face, one eye that's red and one that's green, and a chest in the shape of a triangle. I like to stare at her face because you get double vision without even having to cross your eyes. If I stare at her long enough, hopefully I can quiet the voice inside my head. *Where's Mom? Why didn't she come get me? When is she coming back? Did I just imagine packing my bag?*

I lie there for a few minutes, tensing my muscles, staring at Dora Maar and clutching Sam. Every time I try to get rid of him, I can't do it. Let's face it: The only way I can even give him away is if I sew up his neck, and that isn't happening.

Whenever my mom gets out the sewing machine, she starts to swear. She usually doesn't curse, but just opening up the sewing table makes her drop the F-bomb. Then she tries to thread the needle.

I've discovered that sewing skills are actually genetically linked. Once I tried to do needlepoint. I was making a toaster cover. (Yeah, I know. Who actually needs a toaster cover? We certainly don't.) I sewed that sucker right onto the skirt I was wearing. Ruined the skirt and the toaster cover. So there's no way Sam will ever be sewn up. That just leaves putting him in the trash and there's no way I can do that.

As much as I want to stay home and bury myself under the covers or take off running and never come back, I decide to go to school. Maybe there's some reason Mom couldn't pick me up yesterday. Maybe she'll come today. And I'll be ready at the Dairy Dream.

I go to the bathroom and make the mistake of looking at myself in the mirror. My eyes are more red than blue. I try to put in my contacts but they sting, so I pry them back out and settle for my glasses.

I decide to skip showering. I pull my hair into its usual ponytail, minus the butterfly clips and the curling iron. My eyes start welling with tears again as soon as I have the eyeliner on. It smudges. I don't fix it.

"Morning," says my dad, looking up from his *Time* magazine and Wheat Chex as I walk into the kitchen. "Want a ride to school?"

A whole sentence in a pleasant voice. My dad almost never speaks at breakfast.

"Yeah, thanks," I say. I have early-morning band practice so I can't take the bus. Normally Mom would take me.

As I eat my cereal, I try to figure out what made my mom marry my dad. They don't really have that much in common. Frankly, I think it might have been the whole man-in-uniform thing. Only, my dad doesn't wear a uniform anymore. Though he does a pretty good job making it look like he still does. I peek at him out of the corner of my eye. He has on a crisply ironed short-sleeve blue shirt, jeans, and a pair of brown shoes that he ordered from a catalog—when one pair wears out he orders another exactly the same. I think it makes him feel like he's still a cop. He'd go back to it if he could. That is, if it weren't for Internal Affairs. He hates running the hardware store, but he puts on a good front for everyone else. He used to take his frustration out on Matt and Mom. Now, just on Mom.

"I don't have time to watch him run around a soccer field. I have work to do."

I look up from my cereal, momentarily startled. It's as if Dad memorized every hurtful thing he ever said to my dead brother. Then he replays them to us at random. As long as we make agreeable sounds back at him, everything is fine. If we ignore him or try to disagree, he smashes things. Or smashes Mom into things.

Dad stares at me expectantly.

"Right. Of course you don't," I say.

He gives a quick nod and goes back to his magazine.

Dad is nearing the end of his second bowl of cereal. I take my own bowl and glass to the sink, add some soap, and wash them. Then I open the dishwasher. We don't actually use the dishwasher as it is intended. That would make too much noise for my dad, so we use it as a drying rack.

I pull out the top rack and put my clean dishes inside. Then I notice a glass that's cloudy. It definitely has lip prints on it, as if it didn't actually get washed. I take it out and am about to wash it when I notice another dirty glass. When I look closer, I realize that all of the dishes are dirty.

Shit! I glance over at my dad to see if he's noticed anything. He doesn't seem to be paying attention.

My mom must have hidden the dirty dishes again. She's been doing that a lot lately. She knows that if she leaves them on the counter, my dad will have a fit, but she doesn't have the concentration to actually wash them.

There's nothing I can do about it now. I leave the dirty dishes inside the dishwasher and close the door, praying that there's enough stuff in the cabinets so my dad won't need to look around for something clean. I make sure to straighten the towel on the oven door extra carefully in an attempt to compensate.

"Where does your mom keep the phone book?" Dad asks, startling me from behind.

"It's right here." I pull it out of a drawer and hand it to him.

He doesn't say thanks. He just grunts, then turns to the page he needs and dials.

"Bruce? It's Ray. I'm going to need you to work overtime this week. I need you at nine today. Is that a problem?" Dad's voice leaves no doubt that it better not be a problem.

"Busy time of the year," Dad says to me after he hangs up the phone.

"Hmm," I say, vaguely wondering why there's a run on hardware at the end of September. He hands me his cereal bowl and glass, which I take to the sink and wash. I've barely finished when Dad opens the door to the garage and gets into his truck. I quickly dry my hands and follow with my backpack and clarinet.

Dad starts the truck and takes a sip of coffee. When we pull onto the road, Dad puts his seat belt on. He isn't opposed to wearing a seat belt, just to putting it on when the chime tells him to. "Goddammed government regulations" is what he calls it. I guess he thinks that if anyone is so dumb they can't remember their seat belt without a chime, they deserve to die. And waiting for the dinging to stop before he puts his on is some kind of nonviolent protest, like Gandhi, even though my mom and Matt and I were the only ones who knew about it. Maybe now I'm the only one who knows about it.

After the seat belt comes the radio. Talk radio, mind you. Serious news stuff. When we do listen to music, Dad is the only one who picks. Usually it's guitar music. My dad plays the guitar, but only at home, for us. Or rather, he used to play the guitar, back when we lived in Philly. One day back then we were riding in the truck and Dad put in this CD of a guy playing a guitar and singing. "Do you know who it is?" he asked.

"Brad Paisley?" I guessed.

"No," he said, but he looked kind of pleased.

"Who, then?"

"Me," he said.

"You recorded yourself? That's really good," I said. And I had meant it.

Band practice begins precisely at 7:30 a.m. and continues through first period. Rachel slips in next to me at 7:35. Mr. Sommers is on her in a flash. "Rachel! Where have you been? Let's move it!"

Tweet tweet tweet tweet! Everyone starts playing and marching except for me. Rachel steps on the back of my heel. I shuffle forward. I have a chip in my reed but I decide not to go inside for a new one. I know if I go inside, I probably won't be back. I'll just sprint to the bathroom and bawl my eyes out until lunch. With my luck, a concerned teacher will call my dad to come pick me up. So I just stuff my clarinet into my mouth and pretend to play. The mouthpiece still feels big to me after spending all summer practicing on my E-flat clarinet.

On my way to second period, I pass Lauren talking in the hall in front of the computer lab. I keep going at first, then I stop and go back. Before Matt died we used to be best friends.

She's heading into the classroom. "Hey, Lauren," I say, as if I just talked to her yesterday instead of in May.

She turns around and seems startled. "Hi, Sara." Her voice still has that sympathetic echo. *La, la, la.* I blink hard so I won't cry.

"Say, can I borrow your phone? I'll bring it back to your class when I'm done. You in here?" I point to the computer room.

She nods. "Yeah, of course."

I pocket the phone and head to the bathroom. Shutting myself in a stall, I dial the switchboard at my mom's work. I want to find out if she's really on a business trip, but I don't want the caller ID popping up from my own phone. I mean, what daughter doesn't know where her own mother is?

I will my voice to sound older. "Michelle Peters, please."

"I'm sorry. Mrs. Peters is on vacation for the next two weeks, but I can transfer you to someone else in her department."

"Oh." Vacation? Did my mom tell her boss she's taking a vacation or did my dad call to explain her absence? "I was told she's doing a training seminar in North Carolina."

"No, no. Definitely not. We don't have a facility in North Carolina."

I feel like I have peanut butter stuck in my throat.

"Oh. Okay, then. Thanks very much."

I hit end and release the latch on the stall. I try to remain optimistic. Maybe my mom told her boss she's taking a vacation and told my dad that she's doing a training session.

I take a folder out of my backpack and stick Lauren's phone in it. I don't bother taking the papers out first. What do I need them for anymore? I'm leaving soon, aren't I?

I trudge to the computer lab, and, holding up the folder, I knock on the window and point to Lauren. The teacher nods and must have called her name, because she shows up at the door.

"Thanks," I say, and hand her the folder. I wander off, not really sure of what class I'm supposed to be in. Not really caring.

"Sara, wait—your chemistry notes are in here."

I don't look back. I just give Lauren a wave over my shoulder. "It's okay," I say. "Don't worry about it."

When I get to gym class I'm still the class hero. Jamie, the captain of the volleyball team, comes over to me in the locker room just as I pull off my T-shirt. I stand there in my bra, not really comfortable having a conversation while half naked. Jamie's in her bra and underwear and not looking the least bit self-conscious. Of course, she could easily be on the cover of next month's *Teen Vogue*.

"Too bad you didn't come out for the team this year. But, hey, we've got a game tonight. Come check it out. There's always next year."

I'm thinking that I'd rather put my hand through a chipper-shredder than watch a volleyball game. "I've already got plans for tonight," I say. *As in, I'll never see you again. Bye now. Have a good life.*

"Oh." Jamie actually sounds disappointed.

Mrs. Koster marches through the locker room. "Remember, girls, we're starting swimming today. Hurry up and change into your suits."

Jamie moves off toward her own locker.

I should be relieved that I'm not going to have to suffer the humiliation of volleyball. I actually like swimming, just not in pools. I only like swimming in lakes or in the Au Sable River near Ramona's Retreat.

Mrs. Koster made us bring our suits in a week ago, so there wouldn't be any excuses not to swim. I look in my locker, hoping that someone has stolen mine. No such luck. I change into my suit as fast as humanly possible, give my ponytail a turn, and stuff my hair into my swim cap.

Once we're all dressed, we line up for our journey to the middle school, where the pool is located. Scottsfield High School is connected by a covered walkway to Scottsfield Middle School, which in turn is connected to Scottsfield Elementary.

The windows of the pool room look like they haven't been cleaned in a couple of decades and the chlorine level is so high I nearly pass out from the fumes. In the five minutes Mrs. Koster spends droning on about the rules I think I'm going to suffocate from the heat.

We start out with some "free time" in the pool. Some of the girls sit on the edge and dangle their feet. They're the ones who are afraid of getting their hair wet. A few others jump right in and proceed to splash one another like they're back in third grade. Then there's me, walking slow circles in the water, trying to make sense of all of the different-colored blurs I'm seeing without my glasses.

After most of the period has gone by Mrs. Koster yells, "Everyone out of the pool and over to this end!"

I hoist myself over the edge and go with the other girls.

"Form two lines," says Mrs. Koster. The jock girls fight over the front of the line. I join the girls at the end of the line who are squabbling over last place. We're hoping that class is over before it's our turn.

Back in fifth grade, just after I'd moved here and didn't know any better, I was one of the first girls in line. I launched myself into the pool using a modified belly flop and took off through the water at what I estimated was superpower speed. When I got to the other end, I was so sure I had won the race that I pulled myself out of the pool and searched the water for my opponent. When I didn't see her I was convinced she had drowned. The truth is, I was so slow she had already toweled off.

Today I'm ready to accept my embarrassing defeat. On the bright side, maybe Jamie will stop asking me to join volleyball once she's reminded of how poorly I swim. I took off my watch for the pool, so even though I'm sure Mrs. Koster is keeping us well into third period, I have no proof. When it's my turn at the front of the line, Mrs. Koster shouts "Ready, set, go!" in a voice that's as enthusiastic as it was for the jock girls.

As I leap into the water, I remember jumping into the water for my first swimming lesson back in Philly. My mom never brought a magazine to swim lessons like the other moms. She always watched the whole lesson, leaning forward with her face cupped in her hands, beaming. She never lost her enthusiasm, even when I had to repeat the guppy class three times. I imagine her at the edge of the pool today, waiting, ready to take me away with her, but when I get out, it's just me and Mrs. Koster. Everyone else has already headed back to the high school, including the girl I raced.

When the bell rings for English class and Mrs. Monroe closes the door, what I want to do is crank open the window farthest from her desk, lower myself onto one of the top branches of the oak tree that looms outside, and take off running down Scott Street. Instead, I take out my pencil and examine the free-writing topic on the board: "Describe a family vacation." Give me a break.

"And begin," says Mrs. Monroe.

I sneak another look at the tree. Then I stab my pencil against the page and draw a tight circular pattern along the first line. Next I write *vacation* five times across the second line. Mrs. Monroe says we're allowed to do this if we can't think of anything else to write. The important thing is to keep the pencil moving. On the next line, centered, I write *NYC*.

New York City. My dad took us there right before we moved to Michigan.

"Are you sure you want to move back to Michigan?" my mom said during a commercial break while watching the evening news (required family viewing at the time).

My dad muted the TV. He did that during all the commercials.

"It's probably changed a lot since you were in high school. Just because your dad left you the hardware store doesn't mean you have to run it. We can always try to sell it."

"You and I both know that this limp isn't going away anytime soon." Dad lifted his leg up onto the foot rest and winced. Then he picked up the TV Guide that had been lying on the couch and tossed it at me. "Put that away, would you, angel?" That's what Dad used to call me. He hasn't called me that since we moved.

My mom gave up trying to convince him to sell the hardware store, because we all knew that it really wasn't about Dad's limp. It was about Internal Affairs, his dead partner, and survivor's guilt.

"I can't stand working the desk. At least at the hardware store I'll be my own boss. But I was thinking . . ." Dad got this big grin on his face and his eyes sparkled. "We should take the kids to New York City before we go get ourselves lost in a cornfield."

"Sure, that sounds nice," my mom said. Truthfully it didn't matter what she thought, just as it never mattered what any of us thought. All that ever matters is what Dad wants.

When we got to New York, the first stop we made was the Statue of Liberty. My dad asked a guy in a Detroit Tigers baseball cap to take our picture.

It may have been the last time we were all truly happy.

Once we got to Michigan, Dad went from roughing up gang bangers to selling lumber and screwdriver sets.

Dad didn't like selling screwdriver sets. But for the customers, he pretended he did.

Home was a different story.

"You look like a wreck," Zach says to me in the hall, between third and fourth period. "What gives?"

"I'll tell you about it at lunch." I pull out a five and hand it to him. "Would you buy me a sandwich or something at the cafeteria and meet me at the Dairy Dream?" The one-minute-warning bell sounds.

"Sure thing. Gotta run. I got Fisher next period. Can't be late." Zach gives me a quick pat on the back and forces his way through the crowded hallway.

As I continue toward history, I feel an arm around my shoulders. *Zach's realized that something is seriously wrong.*

But it's Alex. "Boy, you look terrible."

I would be mad at him, except for the way that he tilts his head at me and runs his finger along my jaw. Somehow it has me feeling like I'm out of breath and I don't even mind.

"You okay?"

"I'll be fine," I say. *Once my mom gets here.*

"So, you going to history?"

"Where else would I be going?"

Some kid running to get to class knocks me into Alex.

"Hey, watch it!" shouts Alex. He starts to say "shit" but then he looks at me and smiles instead. He picks up my notebook and hands it to me.

"Thanks," I say.

"Thought maybe you would skip history today instead of math."

"Nope."

"We can, you know."

I look up at him. His wavy hair hangs in his eyes. I want to brush it away for him. Under normal circumstances I would be thrilled that he wants me to skip class with him. Okay, I *am* thrilled that he wants me to skip class with him. But I'm also having a hard time shutting up the voice in my head. *Where is Mom? Why hasn't she called? Will she be waiting for me at the Dairy Dream today?*

"No, thanks."

"Oh." He looks kind of disappointed.

"So why is it that you hate school?"

Alex raises his eyebrows. "'Hate' is a bit strong. I don't actually hate school. I just don't really care about it."

"Why not?"

He looks at me blankly, as if I'm speaking Italian. The bell rings.

I take in a breath and let it out loudly as if I'm annoyed, instead of oxygen-deprived due to I'm-talking-to-a-hot-guy syndrome. "What I mean is, what about your future? What is it you want to be, you know, when you 'grow up'?"

"Oh, yeah, that. I don't know yet. I figure that's what college is for."

"Hello. How do you expect to get into college with the kind of grades you'll be getting after skipping most of your classes?"

Did I really say that?

We stare at each other.

"So maybe I won't go," he says. "Maybe I'll just—oh, never mind."

"Sorry. I shouldn't have said that." My stomach sinks.

He shrugs. "I almost forgot. I've got something for you." He reaches into his backpack, which looks so light it could be empty. "That Stephen King book—*Misery*. I finished it last night."

"Thanks. Did you like it?"

"You mean, did it scare the shit out of me? Yeah, it's pretty good."

When we get to Robertson's class, the door is closed. Everyone is going to see us walk in together. I feel a flutter. I push open the door and shuffle over to a seat. Alex follows me, letting the door slam behind him.

"Sara and Alex? Who knew?" someone says in a not-so-quiet whisper. Cue giggling.

Robertson clears his throat. "Pass?" he asks, looking straight at me. He doesn't bother asking Alex for one.

I shake my head.

He opens his mouth and looks like he's going to say something, but instead he just closes it again and goes back to his lecture.

At my desk, I close my eyes, prop my head on my chin, and yawn approximately once every twenty seconds.

Think. Think. Where would my mom go? To her parents' house in Delaware? Her sister's house in Oregon?

I have more phone calls to make. I put my hand up and wave it wildly.

"Yes, Sara," Robertson says, smiling. "Give us one of the causes of World War I."

I blink at him. "I have no idea," I say without shame. "Can I go to the bathroom?"

He frowns.

"Please?"

"Yes, go." He sighs.

Alex raises his hand.

"Yes, Alex?" he says in a barely disguised shocked voice. "One of the causes of World War I?"

"Can I go to the bathroom?"

More laughter.

Robertson ignores him.

"Cody. One of the causes of World War I?"

Alex: "How about I go see the nurse? I think I might throw up all over your replica of the Great Wall of China."

Robertson doesn't look the least bit upset. "You can try all you want, Alex. I'm not going to throw you out of class. I'll simply send an e-mail to your coach." He goes to his desk and hovers over the computer keyboard.

Trump.

Alex turns and gives me the "I tried" shrug. I hightail it out the door before Robertson can call me back.

The bathroom has become my new phoning headquarters. I lean against a sink, dial my grandmother's number and wait.

"Hello," my grandpa barks into the phone.

"Hi, Grandpa. It's Sara."

"Who?" Grandpa doesn't have a hearing aid, but he really needs one.

The door opens. Rachel passes in front of me in her flip-flops, with hot-pink polish on her toenails. She stops in front of the other mirror, and works on her makeup. *Shit.* She's the last person I'd have picked to eavesdrop on my life. Rachel's dad owns the Scottsfield funeral parlor. Whenever you go by the place it has the name of the person who just died on the marquee, kind of like a movie listing. Her family's been pissed at mine ever since we got someone from out of town to do Matt's funeral.

"It's Sara," I say a bit louder. "Your granddaughter."

Rachel snickers. I move away from the sinks and stare at the graffiti on the stalls. The carving that used to have RACHEL + JASON with a heart around it now has Jason's name crossed out in lipstick. I peek at her again. She isn't looking too broken up about it.

"It's Sara!" he shouts, presumably at my grandmother.

I hear a muffled voice in the background. "Just a second, tell her I'm getting the muffins out of the oven."

"She's getting the muffins out of the oven!" shouts Grandpa, at a volume ten times louder than a normal person.

"So how are you, Grandpa?"

"What?"

"I said, how are you doing?"

"We're doing just fine. Here you go. Here's your grandmother."

"Sara, dear. Shouldn't you be at school? Is something wrong?"

This is the part where I should tell her that my mom is missing and my dad is insane, but instead I say, "No, nothing's wrong. I'm home sick today."

The toilet flushes. It sounds loud and industrial. Nothing like the toilet we have at home.

"You don't sound sick," my grandma says.

"I've been throwing up all morning. So I thought I'd call and see how you guys were doing. There's nothing on TV right now."

Grandma pauses, as if trying to reconcile the loud toilet flush with me being at home. "We're just fine. We've got Grandpa's heart doctor appointment this afternoon, then tomorrow morning it's our day to deliver Meals On Wheels." My grandma is way into volunteerism. "What kind of service projects do you have going on at your school this year?"

Our family is the opposite of my grandparents. We never volunteer for anything. Although once my mom and I are on our own, who knows, maybe we'll start. I make something up. It's easier than hearing my grandma talk about how important it is to help others. "I think there's this Habitat for Humanity thing next month."

"Oh, that's wonderful. You'll have to tell me all about it."

I make one last attempt. "So, nothing else is new with you?" This is the point where she's supposed to mention that my mom called to say that she's on her way to see them.

"No, that's about it," she says.

"Okay, great then. I'll let you get back to *Wheel of Fortune*."

"*The Price Is Right*, dear. *Wheel of Fortune* is on in the evening."

"Right. Of course. Talk to you later, then." I disconnect.

Rachel washes her hands and leaves.

The call to my aunt goes similarly except that my uncle (who works from home) doesn't need a hearing aid and my aunt definitely doesn't believe I've just called to see what's up with her. But I don't feel like I can share the truth. If I tell them that my mom is missing and has either run away from my dad because he's beating her up or that I think my dad killed my mom, they'll insist that I call the police. In fact, they'll probably call the police for me, i.e., Jack Reynolds. I'll be as good as dead. The best thing I can do is to sit tight and wait for Mom to come back for me. There must be a good reason why she didn't pick me up yesterday. I just can't think of it right now.

I go back to class and put my head down.

"Sara, you were gone more than ten minutes." I prop my head up. Robertson is towering above my desk.

"Sorry, stomachache," I say.

Robertson narrows his eyes at me. "Don't let it happen again."

I nod and pretend to pay attention. The last thing I need is Robertson calling home and asking to speak to my parents.

This is what my version of paying attention looks like:

Stare intently at Robertson. Squint at the board.

Write furiously: *Must leave. Have to go. Must leave. Have to go. She's coming back. Be patient. Stay calm. Must leave. Have to go.*

Pretend not to notice Alex's desk moving closer to mine. Turn the page in my notebook so Alex can't see what I'm writing. Copy down what's actually written on the board. Hide the note Alex slides to me under my notebook. Try to recover from accelerated heartbeat caused by Alex's hand brushing mine as he passes me the note.

Stare at Robertson. Stare at the board.

Think about kissing Alex. Look at Alex. Notice dimples. Wonder how someone can look so hot in a T-shirt with a sports logo on it. Imagine the scratch of stubble against my cheek. Try to slow my breathing.

Notice Alex's desk is only six inches from mine. Let Alex lock pinkies with me so as not to cause a scene. Okay and because I want to.

Ignore snickers.

Drop Alex's hand when Robertson turns around.

Read note from Alex: *Have lunch with me?*

Send back answer: *Can't.*

Return to original page of notes. Cover page with arm so Alex can't see and continue writing: *Must leave. Have to go.*

When the bell rings, I'm the first out the door and Alex is right behind me.

"Hey, wait up!"

My heart skips a beat. Let's face it: Alex is hot, easy to talk to, and definitely interested.

Focus. This is no time for romance. I pretend not to hear him. I concentrate on my footsteps. I have this little singsong marching tune playing in my head. *Mom. Mom. Where is Mom?*

He catches up to me anyway.

"What's the big hurry? Besides escaping Robertson's lecture on the horrors of World War I?"

"Meeting someone," I say, taking the front steps two at a time.

"The Dairy Dream again?"

Today I have a hooded sweatshirt with me. I zip it up and start power-walking.

Alex glides effortlessly along next to me. "You want to work on the history project together?" he asks.

Do I tell him no now so he doesn't get stuck doing the paper all by himself once I disappear? I decide not to. It will give him a good excuse to ask for an extension later. I look over at him. *God, I love the way his hair always looks just a tiny bit mussed up.* "You were actually planning on writing a paper?" I say.

"With the right topic, history can be interesting." When he smiles at me his whole face lights up. "Well, and with the right girl."

I laugh and shake my head. "You've got it down pretty well. Flirt a little, flash your brilliant smile, and get the girl to write the paper for you. Only, haven't you noticed? I'm not the most dedicated student lately."

"So now you know I'm after you and not your writing skills."

My heart beats faster. "And why would that be?"

"You're pretty even when your eyes are all puffy from crying."

I lift my eyebrows.

"That, and you're fun to talk to." Then, just like he did in history class, he reaches over and wraps his pinky around mine.

When we get to the Dairy Dream, I scan the cars in the lot, then lead Alex over to the picnic table we used yesterday. Our pinkies come undone as we sit. To give my hands something to do, I open my backpack and take out the book Alex loaned me.

"So what's it about?" I ask.

He smashes his lips together and turns a pretend key. "Nope. No can do."

I roll my eyes and turn the book over to read the back cover. "Hey," Alex says, covering the text with one hand. "No cheating."

"Reading the back cover isn't cheating."

"Sure it is. I never read the synopsis. I like to be surprised. Really surprised."

"So how do you pick a book?"

"I read the first page. If I like it—" He pauses and gives me this goofy grin. "I keep reading." I have the feeling he isn't talking about books anymore.

"Want some ice cream?" Alex asks.

"Not today. Thanks." I'm feeling hopeful. I'm sure my mom will arrive any minute, she'll explain everything, and we'll be on our way to our new life. I wonder where we're going. Colorado, maybe? Or Florida? I'm excited. Then I look over at Alex. Damn. Why can't this be as easy as it was two nights ago? Then there's Zach. How can I just leave him? And Lauren—now I'll never have a chance to make things right with her.

At least I won't miss the house. It'll be good to be away from all the memories that live inside. I don't think I'll miss my dad, either. Because the Dad that I want to remember died when we moved from Philly.

"So, do you have any ideas for the history project?"

Project? "Huh?"

"I've always been fascinated by the Dirty War in Argentina."

I have no idea what Alex is talking about.

"You know, Argentina during the late seventies, early eighties. When the government kidnapped its own citizens and they were never heard from again? We learned about it in Spanish class. They were called los Deseparecidos—the Disappeared."

The Disappeared. How ironic. My mother disappeared. Soon I'll disappear. Only not like the Disappeared, I hope. I feel a little sick inside. Alex looks at me with his head tilted to one side. He's waiting for my answer. "Sorry. Maybe we can try a different topic?"

"Yeah, no problem. You wanna give me your phone number?"

I must look surprised because Alex adds, "So we can work on the project." But the way he almost laughs when he says the word "project" lets me know that's not why he's asking.

I raise my eyebrows. "Right. For the *project.*" I tell him my number.

"Want mine?" he asks with a wicked grin.

"Sure." I pull out my phone and start typing.

Zach appears in the distance with a paper bag in his hand and the sun on his shoulders. I try to wave at him as if today is just another day at the Dairy Dream.

"I can't believe it—all this time you've been crying over Zach?" Alex sounds disappointed.

"No, not exactly." *But you'll be safer if you believe that than if you know the truth.*

"Hey, buddy," Zach greets me. He's adopted Matt's pet name for me. "Got you some tacos." He plops the bag down and slides onto the picnic table across from me, then nods politely at Alex. "Two soft, one hard, beef with cheese and tomatoes. None of that wilted bleach lettuce and no onions. And a root beer." Zach knows about the root beer *whoosh* thing.

"You're adorable," I say to Zach. I lean across the table, hug him, and give him a kiss on the cheek. I take him in, blond hair going every which way, the soft curve of his chin, the sparkling blue eyes, the smile that lets you know he cares. He's the closest thing I have to a brother.

I think Alex must have seen the look that passed between us, that look that says, "Everything is okay now that you're here." I can't help it, because it's true.

"Hey, good game last week," Zach says. "Good luck this Friday."

"Thanks, man. You gonna be there?" says Alex.

"No, can't make it this week. It's my mom's birthday and we're going to some sort of play. She's kind of like Sara, here. Not really a sports fan."

"Yeah, Sara mentioned that she isn't exactly looking forward to having to play in the band at the game."

Zach snorts. "That's a bit of an understatement. Did she mention what she does to pass the time between songs?"

Alex shakes his head. "No, do tell."

"Zach—" I lean across the table and try to cover his mouth with my hand but he squirms away. "She reads *Soap Opera Digest* in the stands."

"Really now? No Stephen King?" Alex raises his eyebrows.

"A book would be too thick to fit under my uniform."

"You know, I'm actually kind of surprised that she takes magazines to games. She's so particular about keeping them in pristine condition. Once I spilled a tiny bit of pop on one of them and she didn't talk to me for a month," says Zach.

"It was only a week," I say. "And it was the *Winds of Change* tenth anniversary issue."

"Need I say more?" says Zach. "Except to mention that she has every magazine from the past twenty years in her room. It's a miracle she even has room to sleep."

"It's the past *five* years. And they have a very discreet presence in my room. Plus, they're neatly organized." That part is true. Because if they weren't, Dad would have tossed them all in an instant. Too bad I can't take them with me. *At least Mom and I will still be able to watch* The Winds of Change *together.*

"Well, this has all been very enlightening," Alex says, laughing, "but I guess I'll be heading back to class. Algebra test, you know, Sara."

I give him a little shove to get him to stop laughing. It doesn't work. "No, I didn't. You study?"

"Nah." He attempts to stop laughing. "Well, I'll see you Saturday night. Around eight? Pick you up?"

"Sure," I say, feeling my heart break because I know I won't be there when he shows up.

"Actually, I suppose I'll see you in history tomorrow first. And Friday."

"I suppose you will." *Not.*

Alex saunters off to school, hands in the pockets of his jeans, backpack slung over one arm. I want to call him back, tell him to stay a while longer. Say good-bye for real. *God, I never even got to kiss him yet.*

"What was that about?" Zach asks in a teasing voice. He takes his last bite of taco.

I shrug. "Some party he invited me to."

"You two dating? Since when?"

"Since never," I say. "I was pretty messed up yesterday. I think he asked me out of pity."

"That wasn't pity." He tips his cup back, tapping it to loosen the ice.

"It doesn't matter anyhow. I'm not going to any party with Alex, because I'm not going to be here. My mom and I are getting out of here. We're leaving Dad."

Zach let the ice fall back in the cup. "You're serious, aren't you?" Zach knows what's been going on at home. Well, some of it at least. I leave out the worst parts when we talk.

I nod.

"When?"

"Any minute. My mom's picking me up from here. Or at least I hope she is. She was supposed to get me yesterday, but something must have come up."

"What do you mean? What came up?" Zach asks sharply.

"I don't know. She didn't come home last night."

Zach looks as scared as I feel. "So what makes you think that she's coming today?"

"She has to, Zach." My eyes fill with tears.

Zach moves to my side of the picnic table, puts his arms around me, and holds me tight. "It's going to be all right." The smell of his aftershave comforts me and makes me feel like it's both Zach's and Matt's arms around me. It's like watching Zach play soccer. If I squint my eyes, the blond blur can pass for Matt, for a few seconds at least. In those seconds my heart is full.

But once I shouted, "Way to go, Matt!" after Zach made a goal. He looked up at me in the stands and I saw the sadness on his face. Then someone tried to pass him the ball. It bounced off his knee and the other team snatched it away.

We sit at the picnic table, not feeling the need for small talk. After a few minutes I leave to go to the bank to clear out my savings account, while Zach keeps an eye out for my mom.

When I get back from the bank, I decide to show Zach my hideout behind the dentist office. We certainly can't stay at the Dairy Dream. Mrs. Hamilton, who is scooping ice cream again today, doesn't limit herself to snooping in her own daughter's life. Besides, she's glaring at me. I think Jessica must have mentioned the whole nosebleed incident.

Zach takes out his iPod and hands me one of his earbuds. Taylor Swift is playing. Zach isn't crazy about country music, but he keeps it on his iPod for me.

"So what are you writing about this month?" I ask him. Zach writes for the school paper, the *Scottsfield Sentinel*.

"Just an article on the new English teacher and a movie review. The one about the FBI agent."

"Oh, too bad I'll miss seeing the movie with you. At least, I hope I'll miss seeing it with you. Send me a copy of the article?" Of course there is no way I'm going to be able to give him our new address, but I feel better pretending.

"Sure thing."

My cell phone dings. I have a text message from Alex. WHAT DO U THINK OF MISERY?

I text back, NO CHANCE TO READ IN HOUR SINCE LAST SAW U.

I'm also not sure I have the stomach to read horror anymore.

"Who's that?" Zach points at my phone.

"No one, really." It feels like a lie, because already I find myself thinking of Alex way more than I've thought about any guy in a long while. But, it's not like I'm going to be anyone special to Alex after tomorrow, except "that girl who skipped town with his copy of *Misery*." If he calls me tomorrow, Keith Urban will be singing from the bottom of some river, maybe the Au Sable, because that's where I'll have to throw my phone so my dad can't trace it.

When I look up, Zach is taking a picture of me with his phone. Zach is always taking pictures.

"Mark my words. Someday you're going to have a picture in *Time* magazine alongside some prizewinning article that you've written."

"Yeah, right. Make that *Country Time*," he says.

Zach hates that magazine. It's a local one about life in the country.

"Well at least they print gorgeous pictures," I say.

"I have a picture of Alex, too," he says all innocent-like, "that

I took while you two were busy staring at each other. Want me to send it to you?"

I shrug my shoulders like it doesn't matter. "Sure, go ahead."

I bring up the picture on my phone and try not to stare. As usual, Zach snapped it at just the right moment. It captured both the smile on Alex's face and the laughter in his eyes. Maybe I won't be throwing my phone into the Au Sable River after all.

"Thanks," I say, putting my phone away.

My mom still hasn't arrived by the time school lets out, so Zach and I walk back to catch the bus.

"Maybe we should go to the police," says Zach.

"Are you out of your mind? Jack?" I shiver. "He's my dad's best friend."

I wave to Zach from my seat in the bus and put in my earbuds. Then I open my backpack and look for the Stephen King book Alex loaned me.

Instead I find the crumpled-up piece of paper from history class. I don't need to open it to remember what I wrote.

Don't listen to your heart.

Can't trust Dad.

Must not tell.

I try to block out the fourth line from my mind. The line I didn't write. The one I refuse to believe:

Mom is dead.

CHAPTER 5

Wednesday

The bus drops me off at three thirty. That gives me almost two hours before my dad will be home. I unlock the front door.

"Hello? Mom?"

But there is no answer.

I grab some Ritz Bits from the pantry and a carrot from the fridge. Then I go to see Chester, the neighbor's horse. He's waiting for me.

"Sorry about yesterday, little fellow." I rub the white diamond-shaped spot on his nose and hold the carrot out flat on my hand. "I'm not supposed to be here today either." I love the echoing, snapping sound of the carrot as he crunches it. "I wish I could stay and chat," I say, "but there's someone I've got to find." Chester tosses his head upward, sort of like a nod in reverse, then he takes off for the center of the pasture.

He seems to be limping. My heart skips a beat.

"You okay there, Chester?"

He stands there, flicking his tail.

It's probably nothing. No doubt he'll be fine by tomorrow.

Back inside the house, I unload the dishwasher and wash everything. I even dry the dishes and put them away, so it's done when Dad gets home. I keep a clean glass out for myself and press it against the lever for the refrigerator's ice maker. Ice thunders into the glass. I fill my glass from the tap—the water button on the fridge is too slow and I don't mind the taste of unfiltered well water. In fact, what I can't stand is city water. The chlorine smell always makes me feel like I'm trapped in gym class at the indoor pool. I turn the stereo on full blast because the house is too quiet. Then I go into my parents' bedroom.

I set my water glass on the runner my mom keeps on her dresser. Everything is neat and precise, just like my dad likes it, except the lampshade on my mother's nightstand is noticeably crooked. I shiver. Did Dad push Mom into the lamp? Did he hit her with it? I click the switch, but the light doesn't go on. I unscrew the lightbulb and shake it. Burnt out. *Should I change it? Better not.* I screw it back in.

Lifting up the rose-covered comforter, I look under the bed. A stray pack of cigarettes is the only thing there. If there had been a fire in the fireplace, I would have flung them in, but instead I shove them in the pocket of my jeans. At least Mom's suitcase is gone.

Just to be sure, I go into their bathroom and check out the palm-tree toothbrush holder. Only one toothbrush. Blue. My dad's.

I open the cabinets under the sink and look for my mother's makeup bag. Gone. Hair dryer—gone. Curling iron—gone. At least her things haven't been magically put away like mine were.

I hope that somewhere there's a clue as to where my mom went or a note that she has left for me. I don't know what I'm looking for, but I look anyhow. I check the drawers of her dresser and nightstand and her jewelry box.

That's when I find it. The locket that Matt had given her three Christmases ago. She wears it every day. Without fail. Weekdays, Saturdays, and Sundays. Why isn't she wearing it now?

I open the locket and look at the tiny pictures of Matt and me on the inside. They're pictures from when we were much younger. And happier.

I want to keep the locket, so I can feel a little closer to both Mom and Matt, but I know I have to put it back. My dad notices everything.

I start to put the locket in the little drawer. *Wait a minute. The chain is broken.* I inspect the damage with my fingers.

It's as if someone had yanked off the necklace.

In anger.

Don't be ridiculous, Sara. It just broke. Nothing sinister in that.

I return the necklace to the little drawer and put the jewelry box back on the dresser. In the same place, I hope.

I try to remember whether or not my mom was wearing the necklace Monday night or Tuesday morning.

Sinking down on the bed, I attempt to calm my nerves. *Your dad did not yank it off her neck on Tuesday. She probably broke it before that.*

Still trying to convince myself that everything's okay, I go and get a kitchen chair and look behind all of the sweaters on the top shelf of the closet. I manage to knock three to the ground. Underneath one, I find a pair of Mom's god-awful navy blue dress shoes that wouldn't look good on anyone. I can't believe my mom still has them—she promised she would never wear them again. I grab the shoes and walk to the garbage can. I am about to let them drop when I realize I can't. Dad would notice. A flash of color in one shoe catches my eye. It's one of those cards you get when someone sends you flowers. Handwritten on the card is a scrawled heart and the name "Brian."

Does the card mean anything? Or is it simply one of the many we got for Matt's funeral? And who is Brian? I put the shoes back and go to the spare bedroom that my mom uses as an office. I leaf through papers in the filing cabinet, go through the desk drawers, and even look under the plants. Nothing.

Where would Mom hide something she didn't want Dad to find?

Matt's room. I walk down the hall and stand outside his room. Then I take a deep breath and push open the door. It brings me back to another day. The day before—well, the day before the *end.*

I peeked through his doorway. Matt was lying on his bed, staring up at the ceiling. "Whatcha doing?" I asked him.

"Just thinking."

I sat on the edge of the bed.

"Do you ever wonder what it'll be like when you die?" he asked. "I mean, we either have some sort of existence that goes on forever, or—

poof—that's it, black hole, that's the end. I'm not sure which one scares me more."

"That's a bit intense. And here I thought you were just putting off doing your homework."

"Nah, haven't got any," he said.

What was it Alex said to me today? *You didn't do the homework because you knew you weren't going to class.*

I finally knew what Matt had meant. *He didn't do the homework because he knew he was going to die.*

I haven't been in Matt's room since the funeral. The first thing I notice is that it no longer smells like him (sweat mixed with after-shave). It smells like the rest of the house, except the cigarette smell is less obvious since the door has been closed for months.

Matt could have been a designer for T.G.I. Fridays—he had the weirdest, coolest collection of random objects hanging on his walls. First, there's his collection of out-of-state license plates. His favorites had been Alaska and Maine—he went for the rugged states. Personally I like the one that says OKLAHOMA IS O.K. It's kind of stupid, but you have to admit it has a ring to it. Then there's a railroad sign that Matt picked up from an old crossing after they tore up the unused tracks. He mounted the muffler that fell off my mom's old Chevy (before she bought the Ford) on the ceiling, and a surfboard hangs on the wall next to his bed. One of those mounted singing fish is by his dresser. I push the button, but nothing happens. I guess the batteries have worn out.

My parents are shrine-keepers by default—my mom because

she doesn't have the energy, and my dad because he's pretending Matt's still alive. Everything in Matt's room is just as he left it, except for the dirty laundry. That's been washed and put away. I look through the trophies on his bookshelf (soccer, soccer, and more soccer) and stuff from the plays he was in and ones that he had seen. Matt loved acting, loved pretending to be someone he wasn't.

I fan the pages of his books (mainly plays, including a few in Spanish) to check for papers. All I find is a baseball ticket for a Tigers game. Father's Day. We went together. After it was over we ran the bases along with all the other kids and their dads. I think the Tigers lost, but I'm not sure. Soccer is the only sport I can stand to watch, and that's only when Matt or Zach are playing. I check in all of the drawers but they just have Matt's clothes.

Mixed in with Matt's coin collection I find a letter, but it belongs to Matt. From his last girlfriend, Shannon. He brought her over for dinner one Friday night. It must have been my mother's idea. She tried her best to make us seem like a normal family. She made a beef pie. If we were a normal family, beef pie would be one of those special dishes that she makes for company. But since my dad doesn't usually allow dinner guests, it always feels like her specialty for us.

The conversation went something like this:

Shannon: "My dad says your hardware store is really nice."

Dad: "Umm, Michelle, why are these carrots cold? And they're still crunchy. You know I don't like them that way. Put them back in the microwave."

Mom: "So, Shannon, you and Matt are in Spanish class together?"

Shannon (looking at Matt with adoring eyes): "Yeah, it's my favorite subject."

Dad: "A bunch of bullshit, if you ask me. How much of it can you learn in high school anyhow? Not enough to make any difference, that's for sure."

Not enough to save your partner's life? Is that what you really meant, Dad?

Matt's face had turned red but he didn't say anything. Shannon had looked like she was ready to crawl under the table. They broke up the next week. I don't know if it's related, but it certainly couldn't have helped.

If there is any clue as to where my mom is, I finally decide it isn't in Matt's room. It's getting late. My dad will be home soon, so I turn off the stereo and go to the kitchen to start dinner. I pop some fish fillets in the oven, then I turn on the TV and scroll through the list of recorded programs until I find yesterday's *Winds of Change*. Julia is telling Ramón that she had a dream she had a daughter and that it seemed so real, it was like it had to be true.

Good, Julia! She is real! Then Ramón puts on his sad face and tells her that, yes, they had a daughter, but she died in the house fire. Julia knots her brow in confusion. *Don't fall for it, Julia! He's lying! Leave Ramón and go back to your daughter!* But instead she puts her arms around Ramón and says, "Thank God I still have you!"

When my dad gets home, he hangs his baseball cap on the peg in the kitchen, adjusts the sugar canister slightly to the right, and evens the blinds.

"Did your brother call to say when he'd be home?"

Here we go again. *Yes, but the cell-phone reception from heaven sucks.* Usually my mom just changes the subject. And me? What does my stupid, messed-up, sleep-deprived brain whisper to me? *Two can play this game.* So I say, "Yeah, he said he'd be back after play rehearsal."

Wrong move.

"Not that stupid god-damned sissy-ass play again! I told him he had to quit. What the hell is he still doing at rehearsal? You call him and tell him to get back here right now."

In my imagination, I run to my room, grab Sam, and fling myself onto my bed. In real life, my heart beats faster and faster and faster and I can't move.

"Well? What are you waiting for?" Dad yanks the portable phone off the wall and flings it at me. "Dial!"

I dial my mom's cell. When the voice mail picks up I say, "Matt, Dad says you have to come home. Right now."

Satisfied for the moment, he stalks off.

I get out the can opener and try to open a can of corn. My hands won't stop shaking. I twirl my ponytail.

"Sara!"

I drop the can opener on the counter.

"Get in here!"

I follow my dad's shouts to my parents' bedroom. The bed is crooked and all of the covers have been ripped off.

"Where are my cigarettes? I left a pack here on the nightstand."

I feel like I'm going to pee my pants. I hope the pack I found under the bed isn't poking out of my pocket. I don't dare look down to see.

"I don't know."

"What do you mean, you don't know? What's that glass doing over there?" He points to the glass of water I left on the dresser. "What were you doing in my bedroom?"

"Nothing." My voice comes out quiet and not very confident.

Towering above me, he stinks of cigarettes and a trace of beer. *Great.* He grabs my shoulders and starts to shake me. "Answer me, young lady!" Then he looks down and sees it. "What the—?" He yanks the pack of cigarettes out of my pants pocket and pushes me into the wall.

"What are you doing with these? My own daughter, stealing from me? What were you going to do with these? Huh? Huh?"

Why is this happening to me? I feel like I must be in a dream, and I'm desperate to wake up. I can't answer. I know that whatever I say will be the wrong answer. So I just shake my head as the tears stream down my face.

Then he takes out a cigarette and rams it up against my lips.

"You want to know what it's like to smoke a cigarette? Is that what you want?"

I shake my head from side to side.

"Is that what you want? Huh?"

When I open my mouth to say no, he shoves the cigarette in and squeezes my lips closed. Then he reaches into his pocket and takes out his lighter.

This can't be happening. I'm the Watcher. Invisible. I'm supposed to be left alone.

He flicks the lighter open. There's a metallic clicking sound and then a flame dances above me. I freeze. He lights the cigarette and I try not to breathe in but it's no use, and pretty soon I'm choking and gagging. Finally he lets me go and I crush and pound the cigarette into the ashtray.

Then he's gone. The truck door slams, tires squeal, and gravel pings against the siding. I can't stop my own thoughts—I wish he would drive the truck right into a tree.

I pick up the cigarette and try to tear it into bits. Only, cigarettes are a lot tougher than they look, so I grab a pair of scissors and I cut and cut until all of the cigarette guts are in the toilet, and I flush.

I know I should leave. Leave this house. Leave Dad. Leave this life. But I can't. Not yet. Not until I know what happened to Mom.

CHAPTER 6

Thursday

The free-writing topic for English class is "Shopping."

"How can the topic be 'Shopping'? Isn't there some sort of alternate topic?" That's Nick.

"Nope." Mrs. Monroe shakes her head and gives a big "Shh!"

I slip a couple of Ritz Bits in my mouth for inspiration and start to write.

> Don't get me wrong, mall shopping is
> great. But the kind of shopping that
> I like best is at a rummage sale. It's
> not like we're poor or anything, but it's
> kind of like a family pastime. Or it used
> to be, back when Matt was alive. We
> weren't those people who'd get up at

*the crack of dawn to buy the newspaper
on Saturday so we'd be the first at
the advertised sales (Dad still got us
up at the crack of dawn, but that was
to clean). But when we happened to
pass a rummage sale and we didn't have
someplace to be, we stopped. We even
stopped when we were in other states.
That's where Matt got a lot of the
license plates for his room.*

My phone vibrates right as we finish our free writing. I suck my breath in and start choking on the Ritz Bits I have stuffed in my mouth. *Please let it be Mom.*

It's a text message from Alex: ZACH SAYS YOU LIKE BIKING. SKIP MATH AND HIT THE TRAIL?

Unbelievable. I delete the message and put my phone in my backpack.

I get to history early. So does Alex. He sits next to me in the back row. "Did you get my message?"

"Uh-huh." Forget butterflies. I think a hawk is trying to take off inside my stomach. Alex's lips scream "soft and kissable."

"So, what do you say?"

Does it count as a date if it's during school hours? "I don't think so."

"Why not?"

I raise my eyebrows at him. "Altman, for one reason." *More important, I can't just run off and play with you when my mom is missing.* I open my history book and prop it up on my desk. Then I pull out *Misery* and put it on my lap so I can read when class gets too dull.

Alex puts a hand on one of mine. "Tell you what. We won't leave until *after* lunch. I can pick you up from say, the Dairy Dream? I'm guessing that's where you'll be?"

"Yeah."

"Great!"

"I mean, yeah, that's where I'll be."

"It's a beautiful day. A little exercise after lunch would be much nicer than being cooped up in here."

"You forget that I actually like algebra. It's you who's into puzzles."

He doesn't look convinced.

"Okay. So 'like' is a little strong," I backtrack. "But I definitely tolerate it."

"Wouldn't you rather have the wind in your hair than have Aaron drooling on it from the seat behind you?"

"You noticed that?" I laugh.

"That guy's got a serious saliva problem."

"True enough, but the answer's still no."

"How are you at acting?"

For the past couple of days, that's all I've been doing. So I'd say pretty damn good. "Okay, I guess."

"I have this idea. You pretend to faint and I'll carry you down to the nurse's office. Don't worry, I'll catch you so you won't hit your head on the floor. Only instead of the nurse's office, we'll go—"

Robertson comes over and stands between us. I pull out my notebook and pen. So does Alex. I'm surprised he actually has one.

Alex clears his throat. "Just so you know, Mr. Robertson, sir, if you're planning on asking that question about the causes of World War I again today, I'm your man."

"Glad to hear it. And just so you know, Mr. Maloy, I have a blank e-mail open on my computer already addressed to your coach."

Robertson starts his lecture. Alex inches closer to me until our desks are nearly touching. He appears to be paying attention and taking good notes. What he's actually doing is writing me notes. He writes a sentence or two, then rests his pencil on his chin and slides the notebook toward me. He also volunteers to answer approximately every fifth question and gets most of them right, so I think that's why Robertson doesn't say anything about our desks. I don't learn a thing about World War I that period, but I do learn a lot about Alex, such as the name of his pet iguana (Fred), his favorite foods (chicken pot pie, Cool Ranch Doritos, and Mr. Goodbar), and his greatest fear (quicksand).

That last one I don't quite believe.

"Quicksand?" I say once Robertson stops talking and tells us to start on our homework.

"Okay, so I made that one up. But wouldn't it be cool to actually see quicksand?"

"Try floating."

"Huh?"

"If you're ever trapped in quicksand, try floating on your back. That's what it says in my *Worst-Case Scenario* guidebook."

Alex laughs. "And why, exactly, do you have a copy of that?"

"Remember when that woman drove her car into the Detroit River? On the news afterward, they showed how to get out of a sinking car, only I couldn't remember everything they said, so I got the book."

"We're kind of far from the Detroit River, if you haven't noticed."

"But not that far from the Au Sable."

"Okay, I'll give you that one. Still—"

"Be sure to roll your windows down as soon as you hit the water."

He snorts. "Thanks for the advice. I think you've been reading a little too much Stephen King."

If only he knew. There's nothing in my guidebook that can help me find my mother.

When the bell rings, Alex reaches over and picks up my backpack. "Allow me," he says.

I'm about to object, but I then I see that all he brought to class was his notebook and pen. "Thanks."

Alex walks me to the front door of the school, then hands me my backpack and says, "Pick you up at the Dairy Dream." He tears off down the hall before I can answer.

I don't really think my mom will be at the Dairy Dream today, but I decide to be there anyhow, just in case. Zach offered to bring me lunch again.

I push open the outside door of the school and follow the procession to the Dairy Dream.

"Hey, Sara."

I turn around. It's Lauren. I wait for her to catch up. "Everything go okay with that phone call?"

"Yeah, thanks a lot."

"No problem." She smiles. "By the way, there's a Keith Urban concert next month by Detroit. Jay said he'd take us if you want to go."

"I didn't know your brother likes country music," I say, shaking my head in surprise.

"Oh, he doesn't. But he owes me one."

"That poor boy is always owing you one."

"And that's exactly the way I like it." We both laugh.

"Well in that case, sure. It sounds great. Look, I know I've been kind of in my own little world lately—"

Lauren puts her arm around me. "No explanation necessary." Her voice wavers. "I thought maybe you blamed me. You know. For Matt."

"What? No, of course not."

"I mean, if you had gone home instead of—"

"That's my fault, Lauren, not yours." I shake my head to chase away the memories. "So, where are you off to?"

"The minimart." She lowers her voice. "Womanly needs. I forgot to put something in my purse this morning. I can be kind of absentminded sometimes."

"Sometimes?"

She gives me a little shove. "And where are you off to?"

"The Dairy Dream."

"Alone?" She gets little worry wrinkles on her forehead.

"No, I'm meeting Zach."

"Oh. Are you guys dating?" she asks.

"No, we've just been hanging out a lot since—"

"Oh, good." She seems flustered. "What I meant was, I know someone who's kind of interested in Zach, so I was just wondering."

"Really? Who is it?"

"I shouldn't have said anything. I mean, I don't know if she wants anyone to know."

"Yeah, sure," I say. "No problem."

"Well, see you around. Give me a call."

"Will do." I wave as she veers off toward the minimart.

Although Mom's car isn't in the parking lot at the Dairy Dream, I'm feeling slightly less depressed thanks to Lauren and Alex and the sunny weather, so I get in the line for a cone. It seems as though half the high school is there, so it takes a while to get to the front of the line. Just as I'm about to place my order, I feel a hand on my shoulder.

"Having dessert first? I've got a tasty chicken sandwich here for you."

I spin around. It's Alex. I crinkle my eyebrows in confusion.

"I'll have what she's having," he says to the Dairy Dream girl, handing her a five.

"Two chocolate cones, then, please."

"Ooh, I see we're living wildly. Are you sure you can trust me not to crash into you with it?"

"I have more important things to worry about," I say, doing a bad job of sounding light-hearted.

"Hmm. Is that why Zach said, 'She told you about it?' when I said I'd bring you lunch?"

The Dairy Dream girl hands us our cones, which we take over to "our" picnic bench. I sit first, facing the street. Alex sits on the same side, close enough so that his elbow sometimes brushes my arm as he eats. It doesn't bother me. In fact, I kind of like it.

"You've been doing that a lot, you know."

"What's that?"

"Twirling your ponytail. Don't worry. It's part of what makes you attractive."

Great. My nervous habit is part of my charm. What will happen when my life is back in control?

"That splash of freckles on your nose is cute too."

There's a light breeze. A strand of hair that had come loose from my ponytail falls across my cheek.

"Do you ever wear your hair down?"

I think about it. My ponytail has become a bit of a security blanket. "No, I guess not." I crunch my last bit of cone. "But I can." I reach up and pull out the hair band.

"Nice," says Alex.

I try to focus on the street. *Where is she?*

"Now that we've finished dessert, would you like to try the main course?" He pulls chicken sandwiches and chocolate milk from his backpack.

"Chocolate milk?" I laugh. "I haven't had that in ages."

Alex looks sheepish. "I have it at least once a week. If you don't like it, though, I can get you something from here."

"No, no. It's great. When we were kids, every time we used to visit our grandparents in Delaware, they would buy chocolate milk for us. The first thing Matt would do when he got out of the car was give Grandma a hug and ask if she had bought chocolate milk."

"You must miss him a lot." Alex traces a finger through my hair.

"Yeah, I do." I take a swig of the milk. "You're right. This stuff is pretty good."

After we finish our sandwiches and milk, Alex and I take our wrappers over to the trash can. "So, ready for math?"

"What about that bike ride?"

Alex takes an exaggerated step backward. "What? You're going to skip algebra for something as frivolous as biking with a guy who thinks you're more fascinating than a geometry proof?"

"I'm thinking I might have liked the jock version of that compliment better than the nerd version. Let's go."

Alex takes my hand and we walk to the sidewalk.

"That wouldn't happen to be your car parked there on the street, would it?"

"Why, yes it is. Don't worry. I cleaned it this time."

Alex holds the door open for me.

"Ooh. Air freshener. Nice touch."

"Watch my next trick as I adhere to the speed limit in downtown Scottsfield."

Shit. I'd forgotten to look around to see if wolf-eyed Jack Reynolds was lurking about. All I need is for him to see me in a car with Alex during school hours. I quickly lean over and pretend to tie my shoe.

At Alex's house, he produces two mountain bikes in excellent condition. "This one's my mom's," he says, handing me a purple bike and a helmet. Alex's house is even more remote than mine. At least there won't be anyone to notice a couple of teenagers who should be in school. We pedal down the driveway and onto a dirt road. Since there's no traffic, we ride next to each other.

"Your mom won't mind that I'm borrowing her bike?"

"Oh no, my mom won't mind at all about the bike. It's the skipping classes that she has a problem with."

"So why do you do it? You never used to cut classes. Not that I noticed." I switch gears as we come to a hill.

Alex stares straight ahead. "What did Zach mean when he asked if you'd told me what's going on?"

"Do you always answer a question with a question?" I'm really starting to fall hard for Alex but I don't want to drag him into the mess I'm in. I also can't say much without bursting into tears. "It's no big deal. Just something I have to take care of."

"It wouldn't have anything to do with that little bruise on the side of your face, would it?"

I thought that I had covered that with makeup.

"No, of course not," I say too quickly. *That's just from when Dad pushed me into a wall because I'd taken his cigarettes.* I try to laugh. It sounds more like a hyena. Alex looks at me and frowns but doesn't say anything more.

We pass my favorite kind of tree, a weeping willow. I like it because it makes me feel both sad and happy at the same time. At my grandparents' house, Matt was always climbing their weeping willow. On the days that I believe in heaven I imagine him lying on a branch near the top with one knee bent, arms under his head. I'm always on the ground, looking up, wishing I had the courage to climb. And the courage to stand up to Dad.

"I lied," Alex says as he looks at the pictures on the wall of our living room.

"What?"

"About the *Smooth Seventies* CD. It's mine, not my mom's."

"Oh. Why didn't you just say so?"

He shrugs, looking sheepish. "I guess I was trying to impress you."

"You should have admitted it, then. I learned to play piano with seventies music. It kind of grows on you. Thanks for driving me home. And for the bike ride. It felt good to get away from things."

"No problem. You sure have a lot of train pictures around this place. Kind of cool."

"Yeah, well, my dad's really into trains."

"Play me something?" he asks, gesturing at our piano.

"Don't you have football practice?"

"I can be a little late," he says, raising his eyebrows sugges- tively.

I play "Wildfire." When I finish, Alex comes up behind me and rubs my shoulders. He plays with my hair, which is still free from its ponytail. Then he sits down next to me on the piano bench.

"You look really pretty today," he says. My heart taps happily, like a snare drum.

Alex moves his face closer to mine. His lips brush my lips ever so slightly. *What am I doing?* I'm going to be leaving any day now. I shouldn't be leading him on, I should be finding my mom. I make up my mind to walk him to the door. Then Alex rubs his face gently against mine. I like the rough feel of his stubble and the musky smell of his aftershave. He kisses me longer and deeper. I want more.

I'm not quite sure how it happens, but we end up facing each other, chest to chest, pressed tightly together, my legs on top of his, kissing intensely, my whole body tingling. The piano bench is uncomfortable but I don't want to move, because I don't want this to stop. Not now. Not ever.

The phone rings. *Maybe it's my mom.* We keep kissing. It rings again. *I have to get it.* I kiss him one more time, then I get up and answer the phone. Alex follows me and winds his arms around my waist.

It's my dad. *Oh God. He doesn't know that Alex is here, does he?* I feel ice-cold. I look up at Alex and put my finger to my lips.

"Is your brother home?"

What is the right answer? What if I say yes and then he

wants me to put Matt on the line? What then? Can he hear Alex's breathing?

"I think he's outside."

"Tell him to sweep the garage."

"Okay, Dad." I hang up and rest my head on Alex's shoulder. "I've got to sweep the garage. What's your stance on manual labor?"

"If it involves seeing you sweat, I'm in."

When we get to the garage Alex says, "You're kidding, right? The floor in this place is already clean enough to eat off. Why are we sweeping it?"

"Just following orders," I say. "My dad likes to have the garage swept out every week whether it needs it or not."

We finish sweeping and go back to the living room, picking up where we left off. I want to take him to my room, but then I would have to explain about the stuffed dog on my bed. Besides, I'm not that kind of girl, even if I want to be right now. After five minutes, or maybe thirty, the bird in our cuckoo clock sings five. Normally I like the bird, although today I'm mad at it for interrupting. Alex pulls away.

"I suppose I should be going," he says.

"Right." My lips still tingle. "My dad will be home soon. I take it you missed football practice."

"Uh-huh. I'll probably have to do wind sprints for a week. Maybe two. But it was worth it." He kisses me on the nose.

I walk him to the door but I don't watch as he drives away. I don't want to see him go. It would make me feel even more alone.

I sit down on the piano bench, blushing as I think about what we did here. I pick out the notes to "Wildfire," close my eyes, and try to imagine that Alex is still here with me.

I get a carrot for Chester, wondering how many more times I'll be able to do this.

"Hey there, little—"

Chester limps toward me from across the field. As he reaches the fence I see that his leg is swollen.

"It's not getting any better, is it?" I say, rubbing the side of his head. I offer him my carrot. "Don't worry. I'll make sure you get to a vet," I promise. "Once you get some medicine, I bet you'll be as good as new."

Chester nudges my shoulder.

I pull out my cell. Even though I'm sure that Mr. Jenkins is home by now, he doesn't pick up. I leave a message.

"Hi, Mr. Jenkins? This is Sara, your neighbor. I just wanted to let you know that Chester's been limping pretty badly. I really think you should—you really need to get a vet out here to take a look at him. And get him some medicine."

I rub Chester on the nose and feed him another carrot. "Well, I did it. I called." *I wish I could say I thought it was going to do any good.*

Chester crunches the last bit of his carrot and limps away.

I go back inside, my heart heavy.

In the living room, I turn on *The Winds of Change.*

Julia starts to remember her real husband, Robert. *This is it! She's going to break free from Ramón!* I give a cheer. A quiet one, so as not to disturb my dad. Only instead of escaping, instead of running far, far away, Julia tells Ramón about the memory. He just laughs and says she's thinking about an old movie they once saw together. Somehow she believes him and she stays.

I wonder how long it will take for Julia to figure out that she needs to go. To get away from Ramón. I hope it doesn't take her as long as it took my mom. Because if it does . . .

It might turn out to be too late.

CHAPTER 7

Friday

The next morning the birds wake me up before my alarm. I open my closet and look through my clothes until I find the two shirts that still have tags on them. I bought them a few weeks before, at the Brookton Mall. It's not much of a mall. It's got a Sears and a Dollar Store and a dozen or so stores in between, including Zone, the only clothing store that carries anything remotely interesting. This is Mom and me at the mall:

Mom: "This would look cute on you."

Me: "It's a turtleneck."

Mom: "It'll keep you warm."

Me: "I'll feel like I'm choking." *Translation: I'll never get another date.*

Me (again): "Check out this purple one."

Mom: [Face all scrunched up.] *Translation: It'll show off too much of your boobs.*

Me: [Twirling my ponytail.] *Exactly.* I can wear the turtleneck under it. Kind of a layered look. *Then I can take the turtleneck off in the bathroom when I get to school.*

Mom: [Big smile.] "Perfect!"

I have these weird thoughts, like maybe if I wear that turtleneck, my mom will know and she'll come back to get me.

I have the shirt partway off the hanger, then I stop. I will not succumb to superstition. Mom's finding us a new place to live. She'll be back as soon as she can. No gimmick is going to bring her home any faster. Meanwhile, Alex would definitely prefer the purple one. I yank the tags off and pull it over my head.

Down in the kitchen, my dad is eating his cereal and reading a book called *Surviving Alaska*. Dad loves wilderness adventure stories. I pretend to read *The Catcher in the Rye* for English class. I've been meaning to read it for a while now. Today I get as far as the dedication page. Then I give up, open to a random page, and daydream.

Okay, I think about Alex. About passing notes, eating ice cream, and kissing in the living room. Mainly about kissing in the living room.

Then my dad's voice interrupts: "He should have lost that weight. Ten pounds doesn't seem like much, but pretty soon it can turn into twenty."

Not again. Dad looks to me to absolve him of what he said to Matt the week before he died.

Don't do it! Don't do it! Don't tell him what he did is okay! But I'm not strong enough to listen to my inner voice. I blink fast so I won't cry. "Right. He should have lost the weight." I stand up. "I don't want to miss the bus." I don't throw my cereal bowl against the wall, but I want to.

In English we can hear the movie from the class next door through the walls. It's in Spanish. When I was picking out classes for eighth grade, I asked my dad if I should take Spanish. He said, "Absolutely not." I guess he was still a little sensitive about the fact that he and his partner might not have gotten shot back in Philly if he had known some Spanish. At the hospital I overheard some other cops saying that one gangbanger had told another in Spanish that the gun was under the mattress. That, and mumblings about an Internal Affairs investigation. Since I'm the one who never likes to cause trouble, I ditched the Spanish idea. Matt had the opposite reaction. He made sure to add Spanish to his schedule for the following year.

"Get started on your free writing, people," says Mrs. Monroe. I shake my head, returning to the present, and get out my pencil. When I reach into my backpack, I find a Ritz Bits pack smashed underneath my history book. I make a slit in one side without making too much noise. I grab a handful and pop them into my mouth, leaning my pencil against my lips so it looks like I'm chewing on the eraser. I consider getting up to sharpen my pencil, not because it really needs it, but because I don't want to start writing. I sigh. Mrs. Monroe's head turns in my direction. I stop chewing and study the board. The topic is "Camping."

I'm about to raise my hand and ask why we have to write about

camping when we just wrote about vacations, but Rachel beats me
to it. Mrs. Monroe just shakes her head and says, "Shh!"

I hate camping. I would rather write about anything else, even
spiders. Like how when I was six I once sat outside during dinner
because I was afraid to open the front door since there was a spider near the handle and my dad wouldn't let anyone else open the
door for me or flick it away. Or how I used to believe those stories
about people who sucked in spiders when they screamed. Well,
maybe I can work the spider stuff in anyway. There are plenty of
spiders at campgrounds. I start to sigh but stop myself so Mrs.
Monroe won't get mad. Then I force my pencil to the paper. This
is what I write:

*I hate camping. I mean I really, really
hate camping. We all do, except for my
dad, who loves it. My mom and I pretend
to love it, or at least pretend not to hate
it. My dad loves both kinds of camping:
in a tent and in a camper. Tent camping is
actually very loud, because you're out in
the middle of nowhere so everything you
hear outside the tent is very soothing
and natural. All the other human noises
that you normally wouldn't notice are
amplified. First, there's the zippers.
The zippers on the tent—Zip! Zip! Zip!
(Center, side, side.) Then there are*

the zippers on the sleeping bags. Zip! (Down.) Zip! (Up.) Times four of us. And there's the zipper of the sweatshirt you have to wear over your pajamas because Dad thinks it's fun to camp when it's cold out. There's the bang of the plastic cooler that Dad closes after he gets out a Coke, the explosion of the seal when he opens it, and the slurping in the dark, followed by Zip! Zip! Zip! because then he has to go to the bathroom.

    Way better than camping is Ramona's Retreat, the cabin we used to rent for a week every summer. We've been going there for as long as I can remember— except for this past summer, on account of Matt. Even when we lived in Philly we would drive out here because Dad liked Michigan a whole lot; he just didn't want to live in the same state as his dad. Which explains why we moved to Michigan after his parents died.

After free writing, Mrs. Monroe decides we need to get into pairs and peer-edit the paper we have due on Monday. Our class is a junior/senior elective, and Lauren's older brother Jay is in the class too. Mrs. Monroe puts the two of us together. You never know quite what she's thinking, that woman.

"Hey there," Jay says as he slides his desk over next to mine.

"Hi. You bring anything with you?"

"The paper? Nah, I'll pound it out Sunday night. How about you?"

"I haven't started it," I say. I'm not planning on still being here Monday, after all. "But here. You can mark up my history notes so we look busy."

"Ah, history. I hear you and Maloy are in the same history class. Word on the street is he's got the hots for you."

"Alex?" I try to sound surprised, but I know I'm blushing.

"I take it that's a yes. Don't worry, your secret's safe with me. Unless you want me to spin the rumor the other way?"

"No, thanks. That won't be necessary."

Jay laughs. "*That won't be necessary*," he mimics. "You're killing me. Yikes, looks like you misspelled the Treaty of Versailles."

"Yeah, well. My brother's natural ability for languages didn't rub off on me."

"Not on me, either. I'm not talking about Versailles. I have no idea if you spelled that right. I'm talking about the word 'treaty.'"

"Like I said, spelling was never my strong suit."

"Where do you suppose she goes every day?" Jay points to Mrs. Monroe's desk, which is empty. "She never smells like smoke."

"I think it's just a social experiment. To see if she can trust us."

A chair squeaks. Another one topples over. *Bam!*

"And apparently the answer is no," Jay says, turning to watch Nick and Andrew, who are on their feet, fists raised.

"Jackass."

"Queer."

I estimate that Andrew has about ten seconds before Nick beats the crap out of him. But Jay makes it between them first and stands facing Nick.

"Get out of my way," Nick says, trying to get around Jay, who towers above him.

"It's not worth it," Jay says. "Forget about it."

Nick steps right. Jay blocks him, poised as if he's on the basketball court.

"I said, get out of my way."

"Come on, there's a game tonight," Jay says. "You know you won't be playing if you're suspended."

Nick seems to consider this. There's hesitation in his eyes.

"You're not going to let Maloy have all the glory now, are you?"

This does the trick. Within a minute, Jay has Nick over on our side of the room, talking about football and other equally boring topics. And when Mrs. Monroe returns, the only thing amiss is the chair that no one has bothered to pick back up. *How did Jay do that?* I only wish that I had learned to do the same for my mom.

Alex and I are both late to history. Me, because Mrs. Monroe kept me after class to ask if anything is wrong since "it's obvious you haven't been doing the reading and that's not like you." And Alex, well, I'm sure it's because he's just being Alex. In any case, by the time he arrives, there isn't an open seat anywhere near me.

A paper airplane hits my neck. The whole class laughs. I don't know how Robertson doesn't notice, but he stops writing on the whiteboard to turn around and ask, "What? What's so funny?" No one says anything, so he goes back to lecturing.

I pick up the airplane and examine it. LIFT HERE, it says on one of the wings. I open the flaps and flatten the paper. *The party at Nick's house is starting early tomorrow,* it says. *I'll pick you up at 7:30 instead of 8:00.*

I know I should just tell Alex that I'll be leaving soon, that I can't get involved, that he's wasting his time—only I don't want to. I scribble *Okay* at the bottom of the page and fold the paper into vaguely the same formation as it was in when it arrived. Then I fling it behind me without bothering to look to see where it ends up. It doesn't really matter if Alex gets the message or not. I have the feeling that if I scrawled *NO* all over the page, he would still be standing on my porch tomorrow night. And spending time with Alex is the only thing right now that's keeping me going.

The bell rings for lunch, and Alex is at my desk before I can even stand up.

"That was fast," I say.

"I had to catch you before you took off for the Dairy Dream without me."

"Impressive. Are you that quick on the football field?"

"Come to the game and see." He snaps his fingers. "Oh, that's right. You go to the games, but only to catch up on reading *Soap Opera Digest.*"

"See if you can catch me, funny man." I sprint for the door.

Alex has his arms around me before I even get to the next row.

"Guess it's a good thing I'm not on the opposing team."

"Guess so," Alex says, his voice raspy. He pulls me in closer, even though we both knew I'm not going anywhere.

Robertson clears his throat.

"Oh come on, Mr. Robertson. You know I'm not that bad of an influence on Sara here."

Robertson does a really good rendition of the "you've got to be kidding" look.

"A man can change," says Alex.

Robertson snorts. "See that you do."

Alex takes my hand and leads me down the hall and out the front door. "I assume we're going to the Dairy Dream again today?"

"*I'm* going to the Dairy Dream."

"Well *I* happen to have packed a lunch. For two. Saves all of that waiting in line in the cafeteria without you. Don't worry. I gave Zach the heads-up."

I shake my head and laugh. "You do think of everything, don't you?"

The wind blows and leaves swirl in the air in front of us. I shiver.

"Hold it right there." Alex lets go of my hand and sets his backpack on the ground.

"Now what are you up to?"

Alex unzips his backpack and pulls out his varsity jacket. He shakes it in the air and offers me one arm.

"How in the world did you fit your stuff for history, lunch, *and* your jacket in there?"

"I kind of left out the history stuff."

"Of course. But I can't wear your jacket. Then you'll be freezing."

"How would it look if I were wearing a jacket and my—the girl that I'm with is shivering?"

"Like you're in a modern relationship?"

"That only applies to things like doing dishes. Here, put on the jacket. I want to see how you look in it."

"Fine." I slide my arms in the sleeves and pose. "Well?"

"Yep. Looks like it was made for you. Even if your arms don't actually stick out the sleeves. Plenty of room to carry a Stephen King novel, too. And it looks like our table at the Dairy Dream is still open. Race you!"

Alex beats me, but not by much (only because he ran in slow motion). When I sink down next to him, he's busy pulling out lunch.

"*Subway?* You went to *Subway?* Please don't tell me that's why you were late to history class."

"Of course not. I wouldn't skip class on a game day. I went last night. That's why the lettuce is a little wilted."

As we start to eat and chewing takes the place of talking, it's hard not to think about Mom, and even though I'm starving, I have trouble swallowing the sandwich.

Alex puts his arm around me, underneath the jacket. "Whatever it is," he says, "it's going to be okay." With him holding me, I almost believe it might.

"Thanks. I hope so. Thanks for lunch, too. And the jacket."

"No problem. So, are you coming with me to math today?"

I take one last look at the cars going by in front of the Dairy Dream.

"Yeah," I say. "Let's go to math."

Since there's no need to wait until after dinner to watch *The Winds of Change* with my mom, I watch it live. I hope that Mom is watching it too, in a hotel room far, far away. Julia and Ramón are walking in the park when a man keels over from a heart attack. Julia steps right in and starts performing CPR.

Yes! Now she's going to remember that she's actually a nurse at Beauford General! She does start to remember. But then, as usual, she tells Ramón. He "reminds" her that she recently took a first-aid course at the hospital. Then he laughs and says she'd always had a Florence Nightingale fantasy.

I go out to feed Chester his carrots. It takes him forever to get to me at the fence, he's limping so badly.

"I know, Chester. I promised someone would come look at your leg. I'm going to go take care of that now. Wish me luck?"

Chester swishes his tail. I pat his head to give myself a little courage.

I walk around the fence and onto Mr. Jenkins's property. His truck is in the driveway. That's either good news or bad, depending on how you look at it. The last time I spoke to Mr. Jenkins was a year ago when my mom made me take cookies over to his house after his wife died. He dumped the whole lot in the garbage while I watched. Then he slammed the door in my face. Actually, he and my dad are a lot alike. They should really hang out.

I ring the doorbell and wait. No answer. I knock on the screen door, then open it and knock on the inside door. "Mr. Jenkins? Mr. Jenkins?"

My fist is poised to knock again when the door opens.

"What the hell do you want?"

I almost turn around, but then I think about Chester.

Talk to him. Remember, you're doing this for Chester.

"Hi, Mr. Jenkins. Remember me? Sara, your neighbor?"

He stares. His face has a permanent scowl on it, even worse than I remember.

"I left a message last night about Chester—about his foot? He's limping really bad, even worse than—"

Mr. Jenkins slams the door and turns the deadbolt.

"And now welcome to the field the Scottsfield High School marching band," booms a voice over the PA system.

Drum cadence. We march out, face the audience, and begin our routine. Sixties tunes. Only Mr. Sommers would think that anyone wants to listen to music that old. Even my mom doesn't like this stuff.

Mom. Where are you? I play a high C and let it squeak. No one will notice one wrong note in the midst of all this noise anyway, just like no one except for me and Zach seems to have noticed my mom is gone. And Zach, only because I told him. We start our forward movement. Our line bows since half of the people are too focused on reading their music to pay attention to where they're going.

Up in the stands, I pull out my *Soap Opera Digest*. Last year I alternated reading and gabbing with Lauren. This year I've been avoiding her, so I usually sit in the middle of the clarinet section and read my magazine. Since he only needs us to occasionally play the fight song, Mr. Sommers doesn't care where we sit in the stands as long as we're vaguely grouped by instruments.

"Sara!" Lauren, sitting where the flutes meet the clarinets, waves me over.

"Excuse me," I say, making my way down the row.

"Hey there," she says.

"Hey there, yourself." It feels good to sit beside her again.

As our team runs onto the field, I look for Alex. "Who's number twenty-three?" I ask. I actually know that it's him, but I want to hear someone say his name.

"That's Alex Maloy. What—you're actually watching the game tonight?"

"I read most of my magazine last night."

The other team kicks off to us. Somebody catches the ball and runs. He gets tackled. Whistle. Everyone gets back up. He tries again. Another whistle. Alex doesn't seem to be doing much. I zone.

"First down," calls the announcer. A few claps from the audience.

"Is that good?" I ask Lauren.

"It means we get four more tries to move the ball ten yards."

"Oh." I try to focus again. The ball arches across the field. One of our guys jumps up and grabs it. Number twenty-three. Alex! He starts running. And running. Players from the other team swarm him and bounce off him like pinballs. He's still running. He runs until he's past the goalposts.

"Touchdown! Is that a touchdown?"

Lauren claps and whistles. I take that as a yes.

"Touchdown, Scottsfield," echoes over the PA.

I jump up and clap too, forgetting that my clarinet is on my lap. It bangs against the bleachers and drops to the grass below. Mr. Sommers lifts his baton and gives a powerful nod of the head to start everyone else with the fight song. I just stand there and try to look as if it's normal not to be holding an instrument. Lauren tries to play her flute, but the fight song doesn't sound quite the same when you're laughing.

When it's over, I squeeze past the kids in my row and go down the stairs. Fortunately we're only sitting in the third row. My clarinet is on top of a napkin smeared with ketchup. I pick it up and try to wipe off the ketchup and germs. Surprisingly the reed remains unchipped. I play a few scales. It still works.

I run into Jay on his way back from the concession stand. Actually, I trip over him because I'm not paying attention to where I'm going. He catches me before I fall and drop the clarinet again.

"Here's a little hint, Sara. When your boyfriend's in the game, you're actually supposed to *watch* it."

"I've been watching. I just had to get something I dropped."

He raises his eyebrows. "What's the score, then?"

"The score? Why would I know the score? I saw the touchdown. Isn't that all that matters?"

He sighs and pats me on the shoulder. "I'm afraid you have a ways to go. Hey, would you mind taking this to Lauren?" He hands me a box of popcorn.

"Sure, but where's yours?"

"I'll get another one." He turns and heads back toward the concession stand.

After ten "excuse mes" I'm back to my spot on the cold metal bleachers. I hand Lauren the popcorn. "It's from Jay."

"If you see him again, tell him it's not going to work," she says.

"What's not going to work?"

"Jay thinks if he's extra nice to me I won't tell Mom and Dad that he was out an hour past his curfew last night."

"You're really going to rat him out?"

"Of course not," she says. "I just want to see him squirm."

"I've missed it, you know."

"What's that?"

"Watching you two pretend to fight."

Lauren puts her arm around me and gives me a squeeze. "We've missed you, too."

At halftime we're tied. Normally I would leave with my mom as soon as the band was done playing the halftime show. She usually comes for the first half so she can watch me play. Neither of us is ever interested in the end of the game. But today I kind of want to see how it turns out. Or rather, I want to see if Alex makes another touchdown. I also wonder if he's going to get any sort of break. One where he takes off that stupid helmet so I can see him a little clearer. So I stay for a few minutes. My dad and I haven't actually discussed when he's coming to pick me up. I figure I'll call him when the game is over. Or maybe I won't have to call him at all. Maybe I'll just get a ride home with Alex. A few butterflies float around in my stomach.

Twenty-one to twenty-four. We're behind. Alex runs with the ball. The next thing I know, half the other team piles on top of him. My phone vibrates. I freeze. *Mom!* It's just past halftime—we can leave like we always do, only this time we won't go home.

I pull the phone out of my pocket. Dad.

"Hello?" I try to sound happy to talk to him.

"Where the hell are you? I've been waiting in this goddamned parking lot for twenty minutes. How long does it take to put a clarinet away?" I know Lauren is trying not to listen but my dad's shouting makes it impossible for her not to. Her eyes get real big.

"Sorry. I'll be right there."

"Your dad?" Lauren says after I hang up.

"Yeah."

"How come your mom's not here?"

"She's out of town on business."

"Oh. Your dad sounded pissed. You want me to go with you?"

"No, I'll be okay." I stand and give a little wave good-bye as though it's no big deal.

Lauren isn't buying it. "Look, you can call him back and tell him Jay and I'll bring you home after the game."

"Really, don't worry." That would only make him more pissed.

I hurry to the truck. As soon as I slam the door shut, my dad takes off, tires squealing. I fumble with my seat belt.

"What were you doing?"

"I, uh, I was watching the game."

My dad makes a rolling stop at the stop sign and takes a right out of the parking lot. He floors it. Dad is driving so fast, it makes driving with Alex seem like riding the kiddie train at the zoo. Each time we hit a pothole I'm sure we'll careen out of control, flip through the air, and land upside down with a smack.

"Watching the game? Did you think I was just sitting around waiting to pick you up? I have stuff to do!"

My lips are frozen. I can't say a word.

"Well?" His voice roars and his furious eyes lock with mine.

"Sorry," I say quietly, looking down.

"What? I can't hear you." The right wheels of the truck dip down into the shoulder. Dad whips the truck back onto the road. The back of the truck rocks side to side.

This is it. We're going to die. I clench my eyes shut. "Sorry!" I shout.

He slows down for a moment and regains some semblance of control over the truck. "Sorry isn't good enough," he seethes. He stomps back down on the accelerator. "I shouldn't have to wait for you. Ever! Do you hear me?"

"Yes," I say loudly, tears springing to my eyes. *Please, God, just let me get out of here.* There's a section in my *Worst-Case Scenario* book about escaping a moving car. I think about opening the door and rolling into the field. I want to be anywhere but here with him, but I know it isn't that simple. If I survive, Dad will drag me right back into the truck. Then he'll be more pissed and drive even faster.

He shakes out a cigarette from the pack on the bench seat and lights it. Then he opens the window two inches. The air whips in like a tornado, but the truck fills with his cigarette stink. I want to cough. Vomit. Rip the cigarette from his fingers and smash it against the window. Instead, I sit there and take it. Like I always do.

As if yelling about my lateness had been a mere preamble, Dad switches subjects. "There are consequences when you don't do your chores!" he says. "Matt didn't stack the wood in the basement so he didn't get to go to the Homecoming dance. End of story. He knew he would be punished. He knew it! Didn't he?"

"Yes," I manage to say. "Of course he did."

"I did him a favor. That girl isn't good enough for him."

Let's see. She was smart, popular, and sweet. "No she isn't."

When we finally get home I feel as if I've been in the truck for hours, though it has only been minutes. Dad pulls up to the front door and stops.

"Well, what are you waiting for? Get out!"

My hands tremble as I feel for the door handle. I jump out. I've barely shut the door when the truck roars back down the driveway, kicking up clouds of dust. Collapsing into a pile on the driveway, I curl up in a little ball. *I want to go home. I want to go home.* But of course I *am* home. Only, home is never going to be the same again.

CHAPTER 8

Saturday

There are nights you're excited about something, so as soon as your head hits the pillow it's, like, *wham!* You're wide-awake and you can't stop thinking. When you're afraid, it can go both ways. Every night since my mom left, I've stayed awake thinking and worrying. About Mom. About Dad. About Matt. About me.

But last night was different. Last night I piled the covers over my head like I was in a cave and did a high-speed rewind to last week when everything was normal—or sort of—and hit pause. I slept and slept and didn't get up to go to the bathroom even when I really had to because I knew if I let my bare feet touch the bathroom floor my dream world would be gone.

"What the hell are you still doing in bed?" Dad's voice rips me out of the dream.

I look at my clock. Seven.

"Half the day is gone already." *Translation: Get up and clean the house.*

I go to the laundry room and try not to think about the smell of frying bacon that would be wafting through the house if my mom were here. Or of my mom's perfectly made-up face—her violet eye shadow and apple-blossom blush. My dad insists she wear makeup even if it's Saturday and she isn't going to leave the house.

I grab my cleaning supplies: spray for the counters, powder for the sink, blue liquid for the toilet, glass cleaner for the mirrors, two dishcloths, two towels, and a paper towel roll. Still in my pajamas, I spray the mirror in my bathroom and wipe it clean with paper towel. I think about how when Matt and I used to share this bathroom it was so much harder to clean the mirror, because he would manage to get tiny chunks of food on the mirror while he was flossing. I always had to chip them off. It annoyed the heck out of me. I miss them now. As I spray the counter, I try to imagine what my mom is doing.

By now she must have found a new town for us. It has to be a place that has more than one traffic light. Maybe it even has a Starbucks. She's probably staying in some crappy hotel while she looks for our apartment. Maybe she's sitting at one of those little hotel room tables, paging through the want ads, circling leads, calling them.

I sprinkle the white powder into the bathtub and turn on the faucet. As I slosh the cloth around, I try to calculate how long it will be until my mom comes back for me. A day to drive there (wherever "there" is), maybe two or three days to find a job, a couple of days to find an apartment, and another day to drive back. So I tell myself Tuesday. If my mom has gone off to do all of those things, she should be back by Tuesday. I'll repack my bag this weekend so I'll be ready. And the reason she hasn't called? If I don't know anything, there's no way my dad can pry it out of me.

Why didn't she take me with her in the first place? That's the question that keeps a constant ball of fear in my stomach. Every reason I think of, in the end, just doesn't make sense.

The hardware store is open Saturdays, so at eight thirty Dad leaves for work and I finally have the house to myself. I put the cleaning supplies away, eat breakfast, and go to sit in the doorway of the dining room, in the crackpot hope that I'll feel some sort of vibe from my brother that will tell me where my mom is.

The dining room is where Matt chose to die. It's been painted, but sometimes I see a speck of something dark and I wonder, *Is that him?*

Most of the time, we don't go in the dining room. We eat in the kitchen, even though it's a little crowded. After Matt died, I thought that we should get some of those seventies-style beads to hang in the doorway so we wouldn't have to look in. But that would have been too tempting. I'd have probably walked through them to hear the clink of the beads. And then I'd have been sorry. No, we should have just bricked-up the place.

Where is she, Matt?

There is no vibe, no answer. Maybe the dead really are just dead.

I think about the card I found stuffed in my mom's shoe—the

one that had a heart followed by the name Brian. Is it possible that my mom's having an affair? It would be hard for her to keep that kind of secret from me. She has a hard enough time keeping my birthday and Christmas gifts a secret, which is one of the reasons she never shops for them more than one week in advance. But since the florist card is the only lead I have, I decide to call my mom's used-to-be best friend. Like me, she ditched her when we buried Matt.

"Hope I'm not catching you at a bad time," I say.

A long, shrill, toddler shriek prevents her from answering.

"Connor, give that back to your brother! Now! I said, now! Sorry, Sara. Gosh, it's good to hear from you. How's your mom?"

I take in a deep breath and spin my latest web of lies. "Great. She's great. I'm planning this surprise party for her, and I wondered if you knew her friend Brian? Because I wanted to invite him."

"What a neat idea—let me know if you need any help. Now, let's see—Brian . . . Brian. You mean, Brian Paterson?"

"Does she know another Brian?"

"Not that I can think of."

"I guess he's the one, then. Would you happen to have his address?"

"Hold on, I'll have to look." Glass shatters in the background. "Connor! Get over here this instant!" There's a loud thump. I think she dropped the phone.

"Hello, Grandma? I broke a glass," a little voice says into the phone.

"Hi. This isn't your grandma."

"I'm three."

I think about saying "I can tell," but I settle for "That's nice."

"Connor, give me the phone."

"Bye."

"Sorry about that. I've got the address. Seven-twenty-two Willow. In Fulton. I don't have the zip, though. Sorry."

"No, that's not a problem. I can always look it up. Thanks."

A few pleasantries later, we hang up, and I start to call Zach. Then I remember he's at work. *Crap.* Who can I call? Lauren. I know I should call Lauren. Except that her parents always give her the third degree when she tries to borrow the car. Where she's going. What she's doing. I could just lie to her so she won't have to do the lying. But I talk myself out of it. *Alex. Alex won't ask questions. He doesn't have to ask his parents to borrow the car.* And none of that matters anyhow, because you can talk yourself into anything if you really want to, and I really want to see Alex.

I dial his cell.

"What page are you on?" he asks.

"Huh?"

"Stephen King. *Misery.* I loaned it to you. Of course you're reading it now, so we can talk about the end soon. I'm dying here."

"Can you come take me to Fulton?"

"This wouldn't be your way of proposing we make out in the back of my car?"

"No." But I imagine his lips touching mine anyhow.

"I'm guessing we're not going to a party."

"Right."

"Okay. I'm in," he says.

"What?"

"I said, I'm in."

"It's okay if I don't tell you why?"

"I'll pick you up in half an hour."

The ride to Brian Paterson's house takes us from one dirt road to the next.

"Looks like we'll get a ride through the car wash out of this," says Alex.

"Sorry. Those things freak me out." And so does Dad's voice in my head. *Don't even* think *of leaving.*

"It's a little cold to be playing with hoses, but if you insist."

"Uh-huh." *I will find you.*

"Is this helping?"

"Is what helping?" *Guaranteed.*

"Is my talking about completely useless things helping you forget about whatever it is that's freaking you out? And I'm not talking about the car wash."

I smile.

"Yes and no. The distraction is good." *Because I'm close to losing it.*

"But I also need to think." *Because there's got to be something I'm missing.*

"I'll shut up now."

"Thanks." *Where* are *you, Mom?*

As we churn up the dust on Mr. Paterson's driveway, I try to imagine my mother living in the plain brick ranch that's ahead of us. There's no sign of her car.

A chill is in the air, so I pull on my hooded sweatshirt as we walk up the stone path to the front door. I ring the bell.

"Please tell me we're not doing the Jehovah's Witness thing," says Alex.

I hear him, but I'm not really listening, so I don't say anything.

"Crap. We *are* doing the Jehovah's Witness thing. Okay, you do the sales pitch and I'll stick my foot in the door when they try to slam it in our faces."

A woman answers the door. Not my mother. I just kind of stare at her. Finally Alex nudges the side of my shoe.

"Hi," I say. "We're looking for Brian Paterson. He's a friend of my mom's. Michelle Peters." She doesn't react, she just stares back at me, zombie-style.

"Is he home?" Alex prods.

"Just a minute," she says, turning away from us. Toenails click on linoleum and one of those slobbery Labrador retrievers looks up at me. Definitely not my type. Or my mom's. Which is also what I think about Brian Paterson when he appears on the other side of the screen. Square glasses with giant frames. Reddish-brown hair. Mustache. And he's short. Quite short, actually.

"Hi, Mr. Paterson. My name is Sara. Laurie Young said you were a friend of my mom's."

He stares at me just like the woman had. "And your mom is . . . ?"

"Michelle Peters."

"Oh, yes, of course. We used to work together. Is your mom still at Essence? Sorry about not recognizing you, Sara. When you first moved here, you must have been this high." He put his hand roughly at the level of his Labrador's head. Surely I had been taller than that. But I let it pass. "How is your mom?"

Either this guy hasn't talked to my mom in months or he's a really good actor.

"Fine," I say. *I hope.*

"Would you like to come in?" he offers.

I start to say no, but figure I should at least take a peek inside. Just in case there's something I'm missing.

"Sure, thanks."

He holds the screen door open. As I step into the entryway, the slobbery dog presses his slimy nose against my wrist and licks my hand. I try to pretend it doesn't bother me. We pass through the kitchen with its dog-scratched cabinets and into the living room, which has knickknacks on every surface. Lots of dog figurines, a few elephants, and statues of kids that are supposed to be cute, but that are really just cheesy.

"Would you like some lemonade?" asks the woman who answered the door.

Now, I really don't need or want any lemonade, but I don't want this guy to hold anything back about his relationship with my mom because she's there so I say, "Yes, please. With lots of ice." Hopefully they have an ice maker like ours that's always getting plugged. We're always having to open the drawer and rattle the collection tray. That should make enough noise to drown out our conversation.

She looks at Alex. "Would you like some too?"

I guess he saw my little nod of encouragement because he says, "Yes, thanks very much."

As soon as she's out of the room, I say, "I'm surprised that you haven't talked to my mom recently. She talks a lot about you."

Mr. Paterson doesn't look away or blush or stammer or try to jump in with any excuse like guilty people do on *The Winds of Change*.

"That's nice to hear. I keep meaning to call."

I leave an opening, an uncomfortable gap in the conversation for this man to say "Just kidding" and call my mom out from the back bedroom. He doesn't.

I look around. Amid the figurines there are lots of pictures of Mr. Paterson and his friend. Presumably she's his wife, since he's wearing a wedding band and he has his arm around her in more than a few of the photos. No children or friends, just them and the slobbery old dog.

Mrs. Paterson comes back in with our lemonades. Mine has lots of ice, just as I asked, which makes it easy to down in a few swallows. It's also just the right amount of sweet, like Mom would have made it. I almost ask for more.

"So the reason we stopped by—" I pause and drink the last of my lemonade while watching for any change in expression. Mrs. Paterson is vacantly staring and Mr. Paterson sits at the edge of his seat.

I start to put the glass down on the coffee table, but there aren't any coasters and it looks nicer than the fiberboard one we have in our living room, so I set it down on the carpet. The dog promptly comes and tries to stuff his entire snout down into the glass. I look Mr. Paterson in the eye and continue, "Is to invite you to a surprise birthday party for my mom."

Mr. Paterson looks confused. Admirably, Alex doesn't, he just nods and smiles and shakes the ice in his glass.

"Isn't her birthday in November?" asks Mr. Paterson.

How does this guy remember her birthdate? Does he just have a good memory or is he closer to my mom than he's letting on? I think quickly. "Yes, but I wanted people to be able to set aside the date. That, and we were in the area for the Chicken Broil. It was good. You should go."

"Maybe." Mr. Paterson shrugs his shoulders. "So when is it?"

I look at Alex. "I don't exactly remember what the sign said— until six, maybe?"

Alex nods.

"No, no," Mr. Paterson says. "I mean, when's the party?"

"November fourteenth."

"Is that a Saturday?"

"Yeah." I have no idea what day that is. I hope that they don't either.

"Okay. We'll mark it on our calendar, then." Mr. Paterson stands. I reach down and pick up the contaminated dog-drool-lemonade glass.

"Let me take that for you." Mr. Paterson leads us back through the kitchen and to the screen door.

"Thanks for the lemonade," I say. The Labrador jumps on me and gives me a big lick on the cheek. I don't want to be rude so I don't wipe it off. As we walk back to the car, the wind makes the dog slobber cold against my cheek.

Back in the car I put my head on Alex's shoulder. One of the coolest things about Alex is that he's okay with just holding me even if he doesn't understand why. Right then I know that I'm screwed. In a few days my mom's coming back for me, and I'll have to leave Alex.

And if she doesn't come back, it can mean only one thing.

She's dead.

CHAPTER 9

Saturday

Twelve twenty. I have maybe five minutes before Dad gets home. Unless he already is. Dad always leaves work at noon on Saturdays. As Alex and I approach our driveway, my palms start to sweat. I don't want Alex to meet my dad, because Dad is always rude to my friends, Matt's friends, and my mom's friends. I wipe my hands on my jeans and sigh in relief when I notice that the garage door is still closed.

"I'd invite you in, but the place is a mess," I say. *Actually, I'd like to make out with you on the piano bench again.*

"Somehow I doubt that."

"I have a lot of homework?" *I've got to figure out where my mom is.*

"Nope. Not buying that one."

"Okay, then. I can see only the truth will do. I'm actually a

Russian spy sent here to infiltrate Scottsfield High." *And now you really have to go or my dad's going to drive up and it won't be pretty.*

"I always knew there was something suspicious about Altman. It's him you're after, isn't it?"

"Most definitely."

"Pick you up at seven thirty, then?"

"I'll be here." *Unless my mom comes back or I'm dead. Either one.*

Before he can say anything else, I jump out of the car and wave. Alex drives a few feet and stops. He rolls down the window. "I almost forgot," he says. "I downloaded 'Wildfire' for you. Here you go." He tosses a thumb drive out the window, then guns the engine and drives off in a cloud of dust. Oh, Dad would just love that. *Please let the dust settle before he gets back.*

I go inside and put the thumb drive in my duffel bag. I'm pretty sure the song doesn't have a happy ending. I decide to wait and play it after my mom comes back for me. I also quickly repack my bag so it'll be ready for Tuesday. I put in everything I'll need except for the things Dad would expect to see, like Sam and my photo album.

Normal. You have to act normal for when Dad gets home. This had to be like any other weekend. On a normal Saturday afternoon, I would practice my clarinet, so that's exactly what I do.

I get out my shrunken clarinet, my portable music stand, and some sheet music from my room, and go out to my pumpkin patch, which is in the middle of the front field. I've always loved pumpkins, so one day at dinner a few years ago I said, "Wouldn't it be cool to have a pumpkin patch?"

"Not," Matt answered. My mom was indifferent. My dad, on the other hand, was all for it. "Great idea!" he said. The next day he was outside in the middle of the field with the roto-tiller. I ran outside and watched, all happy.

He smiled at me. He never does that anymore.

When the pumpkins are big enough, I sometimes sit on them. When they're not, I sit on the wooden bench my dad made for me that's between the pumpkin patch and the skating pond. Well, we call it the skating pond, but it's really just part of the field that dips lower than the rest and tends to flood and ice over. Matt and I used to put on our skates and chase each other on it. An iced-over hay field has lots of bumps. Matt always did his best to catch me before I wiped out, but we usually both ended up tangled together in a pile on the ice, laughing. We'd sit there for a while, talking, until we got too cold, then we'd go inside and have hot chocolate.

I sit on the bench and unfold the music stand, then attach the music with clothes pins. The breeze feels good. I start with the "Russian Sailor's Dance." I love how fast it goes. Next I play "I Had a Bad Day." Matt used to like that song. He left it on continuous repeat the day he died.

"We still going biking, Sara?" Matt had asked, leaning against his cherry-red convertible in the school parking lot.

I'd never heard of a Karmann Ghia before Matt had dragged it home. It's made by Volkswagen, which meant that Matt loved the car partly because it was foreign and partly because it was cute. My dad hated it because he's still against anything foreign on account of the whole dead-partner-Internal-Affairs issue. So Matt had to rebuild the car on his own. Even if he hadn't despised the convertible on principle, Dad wouldn't have been much help. He didn't know the first thing about restoring a car. He didn't even change his own oil.

"Oh, sorry. I kind of forgot," I said as I brushed by him with Lauren. "I'm going home with Lauren to work on our history project."

"Jay said he'll take you home when we're done," Lauren volunteered.

"And you say your brother never does anything nice for you," I teased her.

"It's true. He only does nice things for my friends."

Stupid, stupid, selfish, stupid me.

We didn't actually have a history project. Instead I walked Lauren home, making my own personal detour to her next-door neighbor Ian's house. Afterward I'd popped over to Lauren's.

"Hungry?" Lauren asked as she rifled through the cupboards.

"Got any Ritz Bits in there?"

"Most people don't keep boxes of Ritz Bits in stock, you know."

"Good thing I'm friends with you, then. I see some up there on the top shelf," I said.

"Now how am I supposed to reach that? Jay!"

"What? What's the matter?" Jay said, appearing from the living room, the Wii remote in his hand.

"Can you get the Ritz Bits down for Sara?"

"Don't bother. I can just get a kitchen chair and climb up," I said.

"Oh, no. Jay would just love to help out. Wouldn't you?"

"Sure. No problem." He reached the box easily and tossed it to me like he was at basketball practice.

"You know, if you want to play basketball, you can just go outside instead of playing it on the Wii," Lauren said.

"Or you can wait and play with Matt when you drop me off."

"Won't your dad be home by then?" asked Lauren.

"Yeah, you're probably right."

"Why is it he never lets you guys have any friends over again?" asked Lauren.

"Too much noise?"

"Isn't that a toddler thing? Although I guess my brother does still kind of act like a toddler."

Jay flicked her on the head.

"Ow! Come on, Sara, let's leave Mr. Immature to his video game."

Once we were in Lauren's room with the door closed she said, "So tell me about your 'study session' with Ian."

"I felt like such a dork, ringing the doorbell. I was sure his mom was going to answer. But no, it was Ian. Did you see how hot he looked today?"

She shook her head. "Sorry, I didn't see him at all today."

"Trust me, he looked hot. The first thing he said was 'My mom had to go to the grocery store.' And he got this look in his eyes, you know, like he's trying to tell me something else."

Lauren put her hands under her chin and sighed.

"'You want to go do math?' he asked. Only he puts this pause before the word 'math.' So we go to his room. He's got this basketball hoop hanging over the door, and he shut it so we could take a few shots."

"Yeah, right," said Lauren, rolling her eyes.

"The room was a mess except for his bed, which was sort of made— the bedspread was on crooked."

Lauren raised her eyebrows.

"So I tried to make this shot and Ian went to block me, only I tripped on a shoe in the middle of the floor and I fell—"

"Onto the bed," Lauren finished.

"Onto the bed," I said, blushing.

"So?"

"We kissed."

"And?"

"He put his hand up my shirt."

"And?"

"Then his mom came home so we sat at the desk and opened a book."

Childish, selfish, stupid me.

That's what I was doing the day my brother blew his brains out. I'd been avoiding Lauren ever since, until Friday at the football game. I'd been afraid that if we hung out I wouldn't be able to stop thinking about Matt and how I hadn't been there for him. But somehow that didn't happen Friday night. She'd made me feel better.

We still going biking, Sara? I practice the right answer every night as I'm falling asleep, but when I wake up in the morning, nothing has changed.

One fifteen. Here I am in the middle of a pumpkin patch, trying to make it look like everything is normal, and Dad isn't even here to see it. Where is he? The store closed at noon and Dad never works late. Enough pretending. I fold my music stand and go back into the house.

As I pass the office, I pause mid-stride. No. She wouldn't have. No. There's no way she would have planned our escape using the home computer. Is there? And if she did, she surely would have deleted the history. . . . Right?

Who was I kidding? My mother had a copy of *The Internet for Dummies,* and as far as I knew, she had never actually read it, so she probably had left a clue on the computer.

I sit down at the computer and pull up the history. *Shit!* It's all here: The Wichita, Kansas, Chamber of Commerce. *Really, Mom, Kansas?* A real-estate office in Lexington, Kentucky. Another in Bangor, Maine. Houston, Texas. Raleigh, North Carolina. Eau Claire, Wisconsin. San Diego, California. American Airlines. Delta. Southwest. My mom could be in any of those cities. Or in none of them. Did she leave the history because she didn't know enough to erase it or did she deliberately leave a trail of false clues for my dad to follow?

I look at my watch. I could call the airlines anytime, but I don't know how long real-estate offices stay open on Saturdays. I start with San Diego, since it sounds the most appealing.

"Homes for Hire, may I help you?"

"Yes, hello. My name's Michelle Peters and I called last week about an apartment. I can't remember the name of the person who was helping me."

The woman at the other end of the line laughs. "Don't worry about it. That happens more than you would think. Fortunately our agents keep track of these things on the computer. Let me check for you. Hmm. Peters, you say? Do you remember what day you called?"

"Monday, maybe?"

"I'm so sorry. It looks like the agent must have forgotten to enter the information. But I'm sure another agent would be happy to help you. Shall I transfer you?"

I guess San Diego is out. "You know what? Someone just came to the door. Let me take care of that, and I'll call back. Thanks so much for your help."

The conversation plays out much the same with the other real-estate offices I call, except for the one in Maine. Their answering machine says the offices are closed until ten o'clock on Monday.

Well, at least I know where not to look. And then I realize my stupidity. Just because no one recognizes my mom's name doesn't mean she hasn't called. In fact, it tells me nothing at all, since I can only hope that my mom didn't use her real name.

There's one more site in the computer history that I needed to check. My mom's e-mail account. I go to the sign-in screen. *Think. What would she use as a password?* I try her birthday, her mother's maiden name (Travis), my name, Matt's name. Then I try "sara-matt." I'm in. *Way too easy, Mom.*

The cuckoo clock sings two. Dad still isn't home.

First, I check the sent items. Nothing since Monday. *Calm down, Sara. Of course she wouldn't keep using her old e-mail account.* I start going through her in-box. Forty-three unread messages. There's nothing from anyone named Brian and nothing with a clue as to where she might be. Until I find three receipts, all in a row. Three sets of plane tickets on three different airlines. Denver, Atlanta, Phoenix. None of the cities match the ones from the real-estate offices. All are for the two of us. And all were for last Tuesday.

God, Mom. This doesn't make any sense. Were we going to fly one place and then drive to another? Is one of these cities the right one or are they all meant to mislead Dad? I pick up the phone and dial the first airline.

"All of our customer-service representatives are busy helping other customers. Please hold for the next available representative." *Come on, come on. Before Dad gets here.*

"Good afternoon. My name is Rebecca, employee number 2873. How can I help you today?" Great, I get the woman with the Southern drawl who talks slower than my dad when he's drunk.

"My daughter and I missed our flight to Denver on Tuesday and I was wondering if we can still use our tickets on a later flight?"

"Sure. There is a change fee, but if you give me your confirmation number I can get that taken care of for you."

I read the confirmation number off the receipt.

"One moment, please."

One! Come on, lady, please hurry. Ten seconds. Thirty. Forty-five. I have to get off this computer.

"Thank you for holding. I found your reservation. What is your new departure date?"

Damn it, no! She was supposed to say sorry, she must have misunderstood. That her records show Michelle Peters took that flight, and that it's just her daughter who needs to reschedule.

"Actually, I haven't decided yet. I just wanted to make sure I can still do that. I'll call back when I know. Thanks anyway."

Thank you not at all. My heart is pounding so hard it hurts. *What does this all mean?*

I call the other two airlines and get two other reservation agents who would be delighted to change my reservation. Not one says "You idiot, you got on that flight." Not one gives me any clue as to where my mother might be.

I delete the reservations from my mom's inbox and from the trash, and clear the history on the computer. But I have the feeling that all of this is either too late or not enough to stop my dad from finding her and us.

I look through the unpaid bills until I find their joint credit-card statement. I call, give my "mother's" maiden name and the last four digits of "my" social security number. Again, way too easy. I ask for the latest charges to the account. Since Tuesday: Abbot's Party Store. Dad's beer. Or maybe his cigarettes. Gas. Fifty dollars' worth of groceries at the local supermarket. I open the refrigerator door. Pretty sparse. None of them seemed to have made it here. More gas. In other words, no help at all.

"Just one more thing—can you read me the charges for Monday?"

No airline tickets. My mom *does* have a second credit card. And if I'm confused, maybe that means that Dad would be confused too. At least, for a little while.

I have to find that credit-card number. To know if my mom is still out there somewhere, using it. And if the activity on our home computer is meant to confuse Dad, I need to find the computer my mother really used. I know that she has a laptop at work, not a desktop. So where's her laptop? She brings it home with her every night. That means she either took it with her or it's somewhere in this house. I've searched everywhere—except the attic. I pull the ladder down and am on my way up the stairs when Keith Urban starts singing from my phone. Alex.

"Hey there."

God, why do I feel all tingly inside every time I hear his voice? And like I'm in some kind of alternate universe where my mom isn't missing? Someplace where everything is okay?

"There's a Tarzan movie with quicksand on TV," says Alex.

"I told you that stuff is more common than you think. But seriously, this is what you're doing with your Saturday afternoon?"

"Actually I'm watching college football, but I did blow by the movie. Okay, so I didn't actually see the quicksand, but I did see Tarzan. Or at least, I think that was him. The movie's in black and white in any case. Thought maybe we could watch it together, over the phone."

"You're going to watch Tarzan?"

"How about this—I'll keep watching college football and you watch Tarzan. That way I can keep track of the score and you can tell me if they make it out alive. Or I can come over and we can—"

Rip each other's clothes off. And then maybe I can push the terror out of my mind for just a little while. Unless Dad comes home first.

"Actually, I'm cleaning the attic." *Which I'm beginning to think is a crazy idea. I'm never going to find anything this way.*

"Okay, yep, that's exactly what I had in mind."

I open a box of old baby clothes. Mainly pink. A few in purple. Sizes six months, twelve months, 2T. I'm not even going to pretend

I remember wearing any of it. Why in the world did we still have this stuff? At the bottom of the box I even find some bottles. One of them has a paper rolled up inside. Since when do you need instructions for operating a baby bottle? I take the cap off and pry out the paper.

It's a credit-card statement. Recent. One with just my mom's name on it.

"Um, Alex? I gotta go."

I hang up. I'm not really sure I actually say good-bye. Then I call the credit card company. The airline tickets were paid for with the card.

And there have been no charges since Monday.

Alex arrives at seven thirty like he promised. He doesn't say anything about how I hung up on him. Fresh from the shower, he radiates musk. I'm completely drained and exhausted. Since I spent the afternoon imagining what might have happened to my mom, I'm pretty sure I also have a look of sheer terror on my face.

"These are for you." He hands me a bouquet of red roses. An even dozen. *This guy is serious.*

I almost tell him to forget it, to go ahead without me because I'm in no mood for a party. But I don't want to be here when my dad gets home either. Where *is* my dad? Has he figured out where my mom is and gone after her?

Alex looks so happy to see me. So instead I say, "Thanks, they're beautiful. Let me put them in a vase. Come on in."

I get a vase from the hutch and stash the flowers in my room, where I hope Dad won't notice them right away. Then I leave him a note on the kitchen table, saying I'm out with Lauren.

"So how come your parents aren't home?" Alex asks as he drives.

"My dad is probably out with a friend and my mom is—" A silver car passes us and I scan for her inside. "She's out of town."

"On business?"

"Uh-huh."

"Where'd she go?"

I twirl my ponytail. "Nice touchdown at the game."

"You noticed! I'm impressed. I thought you hated football." He grins and his whole face lights up. My heart starts thumping.

"It's not as bad as I thought."

We pull into Nick's driveway. At least twenty-five cars are already parked there haphazardly. Alex pops out of the car and holds the door open for me.

"Quite the gentleman, aren't you?"

"Just wait until the Homecoming dance," he says mysteriously. He winks.

The Homecoming dance? I envision Alex all dressed up and feel my knees go weak. *Of course, you'll be living somewhere else by then, Sara.* "I'll hold you to it," I say, blinking back tears.

Pinkies linked, we walk up to the front door.

The Russells' property isn't as large as ours—it is only about ten acres—but it's large enough that the music booming from the house probably won't bother the neighbors.

We let ourselves in. The rooms are crowded with bodies. I'm guessing there are about four people inside for every car parked outside. None of this seems to faze Alex, however. There's a keg in the middle of the living room. "Bring you a beer?" he asks.

I've never had a beer before. I've always played by the rules. Done the right thing.

"Or not," he says. "Doesn't matter to me. I'm sure I can rustle up some pop if you'd rather."

If I drink, maybe I can forget how screwed up my life is. At least for a little while.

"Beer sounds good," I say.

While he's gone, I pull out my cell phone, make sure it's on, and check to see if I have any messages. But I know that good things usually happen only when you're not thinking about them, after you've managed to forget wanting them for a while. As long as I keep obsessing about my mom calling, she probably won't. If I can just forget about it for an hour, maybe she'll call.

Alex comes back with two clear plastic cups. Beer sloshes over the rims and onto the carpet. Alex doesn't seem to notice. As he hands me my cup, the liquid runs down my hand. I'm really thirsty, so I drink deeply. Then I put the cool cup against my cheek. The beer doesn't taste bad—just sort of bitter.

Rachel chooses that moment to come up to me. Even before the whole funeral-parlor issue, we never had much in common, except for the clarinet/flute duet Mr. Sommers made us do together in eighth grade. I can't imagine why she wants to talk to me now.

"It sure is hot in here, isn't it?" she says. I still have the beer cup against one cheek. She faces me but keeps darting her eyes toward

Alex. *Right, she's just broken up with her boyfriend and is obviously on the prowl for someone new.* That's *why she's talking to me.*

I'm not sure what comes over me—I've only had that one long swallow, so I can't blame it on the beer—but I decide to mess with her. "Sure is," I say. Then I put my arm around Alex's waist just to piss her off. I half expect him to find some reason to shift position and let it fall, because making out on a piano bench is one thing, but making our relationship public is another. Alex wraps his arm around my waist as well.

Rachel blinks, shakes her head, and looks warily at her beer. I'm sure she thinks she's hallucinating. She's used to being the center of male attention. Not that you can blame the guys. She has chestnut hair like women in shampoo commercials—shiny and bouncy. Her eyes bug out and she does a clean marching band about-face, not even bothering to make up an excuse to walk away. And I'm left with my arm around Alex.

"Wanna dance?" Alex pulls me around to face him.

I shrug. Then I put one hand on his shoulder and hold my beer with the other. I'm still getting used to Alex choosing me over Ms. Perfect. I take another big gulp.

"Whoa—careful with that stuff," says Alex. Then he leans down and kisses my lips ever so slightly. They feel a little numb.

"If I take another drink are you going to do that again?" I ask. I take a drink without waiting for his answer.

He kisses me again, this time a little longer. Then I put my cheek on Alex's chest and close my eyes. I'm tired. Very tired.

"More beer?" Alex asks.

I look down at my cup. It's almost empty. I hand it to him. "Thanks."

The music switches to something fast. I dance and down my new beer. Alex takes my hand and spins me in a circle. The room tilts a bit, but it doesn't matter. I'm here with Alex. We're having a blast. After a few more minutes of bouncing around, I'm really thirsty. I know that I should get a drink of water, but instead I hand him my empty cup. "Refill?" I say, smiling sweetly.

Alex laughs and takes my cup.

"Is there something to eat around here?" I ask when he gets back. Whoops. I'm usually more refined than that.

"There're some Fritos on the end table."

I head to where he's pointing, knocking over a fern on my way. Some of the leaves scatter to the floor. I hate ferns. They always make such a mess. I pick up the plant and plop it back on the table. It looks kind of sickly, but then again, ferns usually do.

At the Fritos bowl, I take a big handful of them and start stuffing them into my mouth. I miss about half of the time, but it doesn't make much difference to the floor, which already has popcorn and Skittles scattered across it.

"Want to check out the basement?" Alex asks, just as I'm deciding whether or not to eat a Skittle off the floor.

I can't for the life of me figure out why I would want to check out the Russells' basement. But what the heck. "Sure thing."

Getting down the stairs is a bit of a challenge since the floor keeps spinning, but we finally arrive in a land of orange and brown shag carpeting. I didn't know anyone still had shag carpeting. I sit down on an orange couch and prop my feet on a polka-dotted mushroom footstool. Next to the couch is one of those fiberoptic lamps that looks like a wig and changes colors. I brush my hand across it. I like how it feels.

"So what's so special about the basement?" I ask. "Besides this lamp, that is." There aren't a lot of people down here. They're all couples. And no one is talking except for me.

That's when Alex puts his hand in my hair and whispers, "I think I'm falling in love with you." Then he leans closer and kisses me softly, sweetly, on the lips. His kiss is both tender and electric. I feel myself rip backward through time. Me. Ian. Kissing. Ditching Matt. Matt dying.

I push him away. "No!" I say it more sharply, more loudly than I mean. The other couples look at us. One of the guys gets up, poised to come to my defense.

Alex blushes. "I'm sorry. I didn't think I had to ask anymore."

My eyes tear up. My jaw trembles. I wanted that kiss. I still do. But I have to get out of here. I'm supposed to be finding my mom. "No, it's just . . . I have to get home."

"Sure," he says. "I'll drive you."

"You can't drive me. You're drunk."

Alex rolls his eyes. Somebody giggles.

"I'll just call someone," I say.

"Who? Who are you going to call? Your parents?"

If only I could. My stomach feels like a pile of rocks. Alex and I stare at each other. There's more giggling.

Then he smiles tightly and nods. "Zach." He says. "This is all about Zach. That's who you're going to call, isn't it?"

"Probably." I turn around and climb the stairs, relying heavily on the handrail. When I get to the top, it's even warmer than I remembered. I put my hands over my ears to block out the thumping music, then I push my way through the crowd to the front door. The night air feels like a cool washcloth on my forehead. I stumble down the stairs to the driveway and weave past the parked cars.

I think about a card I have in my purse. It's this thing the SADD club handed out at some PTA meeting. The one where your parents pledge to pick you up if you're ever at a party and there isn't anyone sober enough to drive you home. Yeah, right.

I take out my cell and call Mom. Voice mail. "Mom. You've got to come get me right now. I'm at this party and Alex, this guy who brought me here, is drunk so he can't drive me home. I need you to come get me. You signed the stupid SADD card, Mom. *You signed the damn card. You have to come get me. Right now. Please.*" Then my stomach is shaking and I can't figure out why except that I'm sobbing.

She won't get the message, Sara. If she isn't dead, she's either lost her cell phone or thrown it away. Because otherwise she would have called me back after one of the twenty-six other messages I've left. I need to believe she's getting my messages. It's that or go insane.

There's no way I'm calling my dad. He's probably had more to drink than both Alex and me combined, only on him it's less obvious. He won't drive any better, though, that's for sure. He'll probably tell me to figure it out myself.

I stagger down to the end of the driveway before I call Zach.

"You're where?" he asks.

"Standing next to the roadkill at the end of Nick Russell's driveway. It stinks." I divert breathing from my nose to my mouth, which helps a little.

"Are you drunk?"

"Uh-huh. I think it's a 'possum."

"What's a 'possum?"

"The roadkill."

"Yeah, right. Listen, stay put. I'll be there in ten minutes."

"I'll start walking. Get away from the stink."

"No, don't start walking. Stay where you are. The last thing we need is someone mowing you over."

"Okay. Hurry then. Please."

I disconnect, sit down on the grass, and pick a stone off the driveway. I throw it as far as I can into the field. There are some empty beer cans and other debris too, but I stick with the rocks, tossing one every few seconds. I wonder what I'll say if someone besides Zach sees me sitting here at the end of the driveway and stops, but I needn't have bothered because not a single car passes.

When I see the headlights of what I figure is Zach's car, I stand, wobbling a little, and back up so Zach won't have to worry about hitting me. He pulls into the driveway and I get in.

"I didn't think you'd actually go to the party. You must really like Alex." Zach knows that I'm just as much of a nerd as he is. People like us don't go to parties at Nick Russell's house. Parties with no parents and no rules. People like us go to places like the bowling alley and drink pop.

Zach rolls his eyes. "So what happened to Prince Charming?"
"A little misunderstanding," I say. "Got any gum?"
"In the glove compartment."
When Zach pulls up our driveway, the house is dark.
"Do you want me to come in with you?"
"No, thanks. Dad's probably over at Jack's. It's still pretty early."
As long as he isn't sitting in the dark again.
I go inside, turn on the kitchen lights, and check the garage. No truck. But just to be sure, I peek in all the rooms. Nothing. He's gone. I'm both relieved and scared to death.

CHAPTER 10

Sunday

The first thing I see when I wake up Sunday morning is the bouquet of flowers from Alex. *God, what have I done? Why did I push Alex away and let him think I'm in love with Zach? Why didn't I tell him the truth? Am I really trying to protect him, or just my own heart?*

Whatever the reason, it's probably for the best. Every second I spend with Alex is a second I'm not trying to figure out where my mom is.

My head is pounding. *Think. The flowers. You have to do something with the flowers.* Dad can't find out about Alex. He'll never believe that I was strong enough not to tell Alex where Mom and I are going. Dad would end up trying to kick an answer out of him.

I stare at the roses, using them to transport me to last night's happy moments. To the dancing, the laughter, the kisses.

Our house used to be filled with flowers. Mom has dozens of vases, and sometimes before Matt died she filled every last one of them, then scattered them throughout the house. I try to remember where the vase with Alex's roses is from. Niagara Falls? Or is it Colorado? The only way to know for sure is to check the log.

The log! I sit up straight in my bed.

My dad keeps what he calls a "log"—basically a date-oriented record of events. It's a journal minus any emotional component, or at least any that he shares with the rest of us. He refers to it whenever anyone has questions like, "Who remembers what we did on that vacation to Colorado?" Then he pulls out the old log and reads it to us: "Camped in woods by river. Went horseback riding in the a.m. Lunch cooked by guide. Purchased tickets for scenic railway for following day."

The logs are in spiral notebooks, a new one for each year. They're all locked in a trunk in the basement in my dad's train room. All except for the current year, that is. Dad keeps that one in his office at the hardware store for making his daily entries. If my Dad truly believes that my mom is on a business trip, he would have recorded it in his log. If he knows she isn't, well, he wouldn't exactly lie to himself in his own log, would he?

"Matt! Sara! Wake up!" My dad's voice thunders down the hallway.

I grab the vase and shove it under the bed. It makes a slight thunk. *As long as the water doesn't come spilling out where Dad can see it.*

"What was that?" My dad bangs open my door. He's already dressed.

I think fast. "I knocked a book I was reading off the night-stand." *Can he smell the roses?*

"Which one?"

"This one." I hold up *The Catcher in the Rye.*

"Haven't you been reading that all week?"

I swallow. "Rereading. We have a test Monday."

"What the hell are you still doing with this?" He picks Sam up from the bottom of my bed.

I reach to take him back.

"It looks pathetic." He squishes Sam under his arm. "Tell Matt to trim the bushes. I'm leaving for work."

"I—I still like him." *And you gave him to me.*

"You're sixteen years old. Grow up." He stalks out of my room. "Don't forget to put another trash bag in the garbage can." And just like that, Sam is on his way to the Dumpster at the hardware store, where Dad takes all our garbage. My stomach feels hollow.

Outside, Dad has set the electric trimmer and clippers on the front porch. I don't exactly mind trimming the bushes—except for the whole *Mom, where are you, Mom, where are you, Mom, where are you* recording that is playing in my brain. Now I won't even have Sam to hold on to at night. Why *did* I need a stuffed dog at age sixteen? I got Sam for Christmas when I was five. There was one last present under the tree.

"It's for you, Sara," my mom said. She handed me a plain white box with a blue bow. I flung the cover off, stuck my hands inside and pulled out an adorable stuffed dog. I squeezed it tight and planted a kiss on the tip of his nose.

"I love him! Thank you so much, Mom!" She smiled and shook her head.

"Don't thank me, thank your dad. He picked it out."

Even at that age I knew that Mom did most of the shopping, so knowing Dad had chosen him made the stuffed dog extra special. I ran over to Dad and jumped into his lap. "Wow," I said.

He laughed and tousled my hair. "It was a long and difficult search, but when I saw him, I knew he was for you, angel. Whatcha gonna name him?" asked Dad.

"I don't know. What do you think?"

"Sam," he said. "I think he looks like a Sam."

"You're right! Hi, Sam!" I petted Sam's head and snuggled next to Dad.

Lately, when Dad did something that hurt one of us, I would think about that day and I would remember him the way he used to be. The way I believed he could be again someday.

Somewhere between last Tuesday and today, I stopped believing.

Chester grazes near the fence while I'm trimming. Every once in a while I look up and watch him. He hardly moves, and when he does, he's limping badly.

I go in and call Mrs. Harper, the lady with the horse stable.

"Hi. This is Sara Peters. My brother and I used to ride horses over at your place sometimes. We just ran into each other again at the library the other day?"

"Right. Of course, Sara. What's up?"

"The thing is, I know someone who—there's this horse that . . ." I sigh. "It's kind of a long story, but there's someone I know who has an old horse that they don't really want anymore. I hoped you might know someone who would be interested in taking it in. Someone not in the glue-manufacturing business, that is. And it needs to be soon, really soon. Because he's got this bad limp that his owner hasn't done anything about." I fill in the rest of the details I know about Chester.

"Hmm. Let me see what I can do. How about I check around and give you a call back?"

Just as I hang up, Keith Urban starts singing from my cell. I'll have to get a new ringtone for my next phone, because I'll never be able to hear that song again without thinking of Alex.

"Hi, Alex," I say softly.

"I don't care if you're mad at me. I'm coming over to see you." His voice is gentle, pleading. *Dear, sweet, Alex. God, I love you.*

"Actually, now's not a good time. I'm on my way out." I try to sound businesslike. My voice cracks.

"Where're you headed?"

I hesitate. This is it. I need to either tell Alex everything or let him go. "I'm going to the movies. With Zach." I use my cold voice. My pseudo-Dad voice.

"Zach. Him, again." It's hurt that I hear.

"Yeah." I don't explain that Zach is like my replacement brother, how going to the movies is just part of the way we cope. Because in the end, I'm going to be leaving. And everyone knows that if you don't want to be found by the wrong person, you can't even tell the right one where you're going. As soon as I find my mom, I'm going to have to disappear, and I can't have Alex looking for me.

"So you're telling me that me and you, these past few days, it meant nothing?" His voice cracks too and my heart breaks.

It's meant everything. "Yeah, I guess so," I say, and I hang up before I can change my mind.

Zach and I go to the movies in Brookton. I don't really watch the film. The banker-turned FBI-agent is definitely hot, but I have no idea what actually happens. Images flicker in front of me, but I don't really see them. Different images flash through my brain. Me, age six, a worm in one hand, a fishing pole in the other, next to my dad. Walking across the entire span of the Mackinac Bridge on Labor Day with Matt and my parents. Snowboarding with Matt at Boyne. Matt's funeral. Mom crying. Dad already wandering around by himself, talking to nonexistent people in corners. Dad's "logs."

The credits roll.

"I, um—I need to stop by the hardware store," I say, standing up. "If you can just drop me off, I'll meet you back at Zelda's Diner."

"Drop you off? I'll just wait for you. But isn't the store closed?"

I look around to make sure none of my dad's spies are lurking among the theatergoers. "Yeah, I need to look for something." I clear my throat.

Zach lifts his eyebrows but keeps quiet until we're inside the car. "Look for what?"

"My dad's logs. I need to know if he's written anything about Mom. Look, Zach, I don't want you in the middle of this. I shouldn't have told you."

"Don't be sorry. I want to help."

"But if my dad finds out we've been at his store . . . It's better if I go alone."

"I'm coming with you. Let me do this, Sara. I wasn't there for Matt, but I can be here for you."

"You can't blame yourself for Matt. He made his own choices."

"But it's okay for you to blame yourself?"

"I'm trying not to."

"And I'm going with you."

The hardware store is also in Brookton, halfway between the mall and the first farm on the way out of town. It isn't the best location (that would be the strip between the mall and Pizza Hut), but it isn't bad. It's perfect for what Zach and I are about to do—break in, that is.

If you think about it, we aren't exactly breaking in. I have the key on my keychain because Dad had them made for all of us when he first got the store. And I know the alarm code. Or, at least, I hope I do.

There's just one thing I have to do before we go inside. "Mind if I do a little Dumpster diving first?"

Zach narrows his eyes and shrugs. "Sure, if you think it will help."

I lead him around the back of the building and peer into the Dumpster. "Great." I groan. "Looks like this was recently emptied."

"Is that a problem?"

"It means that the bag I need is all the way at the bottom. I'm going to have to climb in."

"I'll do it," says Zach.

"I got it," I insist. "Hold my purse?"

Zach rolls his eyes and holds it as far away from his body as he can.

I pull myself up until I can bend at my waist into the Dumpster. I try to imagine I'm on the monkey bars. The stench of rotting tuna reminds me that I'm not. I swing my legs over the side and jump in, landing on something squishy. The bags are all very efficiently double-knotted. Dad's signature. I try to undo the first one. Then I just give up and rip. I get spaghetti sauce and a few noodles on my foot. That was supposed to be our last meal together. I try another bag. Sawdust and shards of wood. When I open the third bag, Sam's ear flops out. He's been sitting in a bed of cigarette ashes, but I brush him off and hug him anyway. "I'll decide when I'm ready to get rid of you," I whisper. Then I carry him over to the side of the bin. "Catch?"

"You've got to be kidding."

I wait for Zach to drop my purse and hold up his arms so I can see them over the edge of the Dumpster. Then I send Sam in an arc through the air. His long ears fly upward in the wind. Matt and I used to love to watch him fly for just that reason.

As soon as I climb out of the Dumpster, Zach hands Sam back to me. I tuck him under my arm as we walk around to the front of the hardware store. I unlock the door with my key and we step inside.

Beep. Beep. Beep. The alarm nags me for the code. Is it 2791 or 2971? I try 2791. RETRY. My palms start to sweat. I wipe them on my pants. 2971. The beeping stops.

"You had me worried for a minute," Zach says, looking pale.

"You and me both."

"Should we lock the door?" asks Zach.

"Nah. The closed sign is up. This shouldn't take long, anyhow."

I walk down an aisle filled with bins of nails, screws, and bolts. I pick up a handful and let them fall through my fingers to hear the clinking sound. Then I remember I've just been Dumpster diving and go to the bathroom to wash my hands.

I dry my hands on a paper towel. "Can you look behind the counter?" I ask. "I'm going to check out the office."

The microwave is the first thing you see as you enter the office. There's a splatter of spaghetti sauce on the top of it. It's small. Not everyone would have noticed. Except for Dad. Dad really should have noticed and wiped it off. I glance up. For a second I think I see a spot on the wall too, a red spot, like spaghetti sauce. Or blood. But I know it's just a trick my mind is playing on me. Kind of like how if you stare at something for a long time and then look at a white wall, you can still see the image, if only for a few seconds.

This time when I shake my head to make the spots go away, they disappear from the wall but not from my mind. In my mind, Dad has a paper towel in one hand and a bottle of bleach in the other and he's spraying the wall and wiping it, but there is still a little speck of blood on the wall. I know I need to get up and run out of here. Now.

"What are you staring at?"

I jump, but it's only Zach standing behind me.

"Nothing," I say, going over to sit at the desk. "Can you check the filing cabinet?"

A coffee mug sits on top of the desk alongside three neatly arranged stacks of unopened mail. Dad must have been really busy at the store lately. *Too busy to open the mail?* I feel weird opening the desk drawers. Kind of like I'm walking in on someone naked. But there really isn't much there except for a gallon-size freezer bag of rubber bands. I don't think I could use that many rubber bands in my whole lifetime. The only other thing in the top drawer is a scrap of paper with the number 362947 and the name "Carter." Is it a phone number? If so, it's missing a digit. I feel like I've heard that name before, but I don't know when or why. I copy it down on a sticky note and stick it in my purse.

"Find anything?" Zach asks.

"Not yet. Does 'Carter' mean anything to you?"

"No. I'm not doing much better over here, either. A bunch of brochures and files in the top. Looks like giveaways in this drawer—rulers, tape measures, mini-screwdriver sets."

He slams the drawer shut and opens the last one. "Uh, I think this might be it."

I cross the room and peer into the drawer. A pint of Jack Daniels. And next to it, a thick navy blue notebook. Dad's log. It's a bit like the notebook Dad used to carry around when he was a cop, only steno-size with the spiral on the left. Dad's logs all look exactly the same except for the year, which he prints on the cover's top right-hand corner.

I reach for it, then jerk my hand back.

Clean! Are your hands clean, Sara? Of course they are. Stop freaking out. I just washed them after rescuing Sam. I reach back into the drawer, and slowly pull out the log. My heart pounds. I've never looked in Dad's log. No one has. I carry it carefully to the desk and sit. Taking a deep breath, I open it and turn the pages. Most seem to be rather mundane entries about lumber orders and meals. Then I get to Tuesday, the day Mom disappeared.

There's nothing. Just a blank page. The entries stop there. My dad, who never misses an entry, has not made one in nearly a week. My ears buzz and I get the same scared taste in my mouth that I get when I hear my dad's truck door slam and I realize that there is something I've forgotten to do before he got home.

I turn the page, and then the next and the next, just to make sure.

Slow down, Sara! Don't bend the pages! There must be a logical explanation, just slow down and think!

"What? What's the matter?" Zach comes over and puts his arm on my shoulder.

"There are no—there are no more entries." I keep turning, blank page after blank page.

Slam! A car door! Or is it a truck? *Please don't let it be a truck!*

Zach and I both freeze like rabbits. "Oh my God, is that him? Is he here?"

Shit! Move, Sara, move! I close the log and slide it back into the filing cabinet. Had it been touching the right side or the left? Right. No, left. My dad will expect it to shift a little when he opens and closes the drawer, won't he? I try to close the cabinet quietly, but it still makes a reverberating clang. *Hide, run, or confront? Hide, run, or confront?* I want to crawl inside the filing cabinet, even though I know I won't fit.

"What do we do? What do we do? Do we go out the back door?" I look to Zach for answers. His eyes get big.

Do we try to make it to the car? Or do we forget the car, go out the back door, and just run? *God, why did the store have to be so far out of town?* There's too much open space! Either way we're screwed. Dad knows the make, model, and license-plate number of all of our friends' cars. He'll know it's Zach's car in the parking lot before he even comes in the building.

"Okay, what are we doing here? Why are we here? What possible reason can we have for being here?" I stammer, my heart thudding.

"Birthday? Your Dad's birthday? Decorating for his birthday?" Zach suggests frantically.

"No, won't work. July."

"You needed something for the yard. Something so you can fix up the yard?" Zach's talking even faster now.

"Shovel. Rake. Hoe. Sprinkler. Trimmer. Shit. Just look. Is it him?"

Zach peeks around the doorframe. "It's the cops."

"Oh God. Now what?"

"Take a deep breath and act natural," Zach says. "Remember, it's your dad's store. You have the keys." He says it like he's trying to convince himself, too.

Yes, my dad's store. *Just please don't let them call him.*

We go into the main part of the store.

The door opens. The officer doesn't have his gun drawn, but his hand hovers over the holster. "Afternoon," he says, looking us over. "This store's supposed to be closed. Can you tell me what you kids are doing here, please?"

"My dad—Ray Peters—owns the store. He sent us here to pick up a paper he forgot. This is my friend, Zach."

"Afternoon, Officer."

"You have any ID?" he asks, turning to me.

"In my purse."

"Go ahead and get it out."

I fumble through my purse, hands shaking. I find my license and take it out.

"So you're Ray's daughter," he says. "Sorry to frighten you. I was driving by and saw a car I didn't recognize here after hours."

"No problem. I'm sure my dad would appreciate your checking." *Is there any cop in the whole county that my dad isn't friends with?* I put my wallet back in my purse. "We were just leaving." I take a step forward, then freeze in midstride. *Sam!* He's still in the office!

"I left—I just gotta get—something out of the office."

Too bad Sam isn't going to fit in my purse. I take my time returning to the front of the store. The officer is still there.

"It's for—it belongs to my little cousin," I say, gesturing to my stuffed dog. "Let me just set the alarm and we'll be off."

The officer holds the door open for us.

I flip off the lights and try to set the alarm while my hands are shaking. *Beep.* It's set. I pull the door closed, insert my key, and turn. Then I make a big show of testing the knob to make sure it's locked.

Our feet crunch against the gravel as we walk to the car.

"Thanks again, Officer," I call out just before slamming the door. He doesn't answer, but at least he doesn't try to stop us. He just stands there and watches us pull away, his arms folded.

"That was close," Zach says, sounding relieved. He shakes his head and turns on the radio. "You think that guy's going to call your dad?"

I pull my seat belt tighter and squeeze Sam to my chest. "I'm doing my best not to think about that."

My dad completely flipped out over the glass of water on his dresser and the pack of cigarettes in my pocket.

If he finds out I was at his store without his permission . . .

That I was looking at his log . . .

I'll be in trouble.

A-trip-to-the-hospital kind of trouble.

Maybe even dead.

CHAPTER 11

Monday

Monday morning I ask Zach to walk me to history. Alex is standing outside the door. When he sees us together his jaw tightens and he shakes his head. Then he takes off.

"Are you sure you know what you're doing?" Zach asks, raising his eyebrows.

"No," I say. "Not at all."

I didn't do as good of a job trimming the bushes yesterday as Matt would have done. A few stray branches poke out. I'm about to go out to the barn for the clippers when I remember that I never put them back. *Good thing Dad didn't notice. Where are they?*

Think.

There they are, tucked behind a bush. I clip the problem areas, then trudge out to the barn to put them away.

As I open the side door, a bird flaps its wings and crashes into a wall. I leave the door open, hoping it will fly out. *Bam!* The bird crashes into the superclean tractor (Dad washes it after every use). Poor thing.

I scan the pegboards and the tools hanging on them, looking for the gap where my clippers should go.

I find the spot. But there's another empty spot near it. My dad's very neat with his tools. Meticulous, even. For one to be missing is a bit odd. I try to figure out what it could be. Plastic rake. Metal rake. Hoe. Saw. Ax. Hatchet. Pitchfork. Post-hole digger. What's missing? I stand in front of the empty spot. As if that will help me remember.

Prickles spread across my arms. Shovel. The shovel is missing. Wooden handle, black scooping part that looks like a Teflon pan. It should be here.

The gravel crunches and the truck door slams. I freeze. Maybe Dad won't notice that the barn door is open.

No such luck.

"What are you staring at?"

Oh God. "I—I'm, uh—I'm looking for the peg for the clippers."

"It's right in front of your face."

"Oh," I say. I hear my own voice shake.

"Put it back and get out of here." My dad doesn't like people messing with his tools or his barn, for that matter.

I stretch on my tiptoes and try to hang up the clippers. Instead I manage to knock the peg onto the floor.

Dad stands with his arms folded as I replace the peg and the clippers. The bird flutters into a shelf. Nervous, just like me. As we walk out the side door, Dad slams it shut behind us. I want to tell him about the bird but figure I better not.

Inside the house, I keep thinking about the missing shovel. Where is it? In my mind, I see images of my dad, the shovel in his hand, digging. Picking my mom up in his arms and lowering her into the ground, sprinkling dirt over her body. I shudder. I have to snap out of it and start making dinner.

I turn on the oven and thaw some ground beef for tacos. Does beef always look this bloody? *Stop it, Sara!* There's bound to be a logical explanation for the missing shovel, one that doesn't involve my mother.

As we sit down to dinner, Dad once again asks, "Where's Matt? He's not at that goddamned play rehearsal again, is he?"

Let's see. The last time I told my dad that Matt was at play rehearsal, I ended up making a long-distance call to heaven. I wasn't going there again.

"No," I say. "He quit."

Dad smiles, which is weird. I should try changing the past more often.

"So where is he?"

Crap. Now what was I supposed to say? Matt loved being in plays. And basically Dad was okay with that. Except for Matt's last play. Dad insisted that Matt quit a week before opening night.

Matt didn't. He killed himself instead.

I think about telling Dad that Matt is at soccer practice. That should be safe. Then I have a better idea.

"He said something about a program Jack Reynolds told him about—some kind of seminar about the police academy."

Dad buys it. "Hmm," he says. "Sounds good." Then he tells me that the tacos taste great.

The phone rings. It's Mrs. Harper, from the riding stable. My heart beats faster.

"I've found someone who will take that horse we talked about. If you give me the address, I'll arrange for a horse trailer to pick him up."

I'm thrilled for Chester, but a little anxious for me, since it means I have to go see Mr. Jenkins again.

My dad's in the basement with his trains, so I shout down that I'm going for a walk.

I stop at the barn and open the side door, hoping the bird that is trapped inside will find his way out, then I make my way over to Chester. He's limping so badly I want to cry. I blow him a kiss and cross over onto the neighbor's property.

Amazingly, Mr. Jenkins opens the door after just one ring of the doorbell. "About your horse . . . I know someone who would be interested in taking him—" He starts to close the door.

This is what I shout at him in my head: *If you don't let him go, I'll report you to Animal Cruelty!*

Here are the words I actually say: "They'll pay."

The truth is that the only "they" who will pay is me. I fan some of the money I'd cleared out of my savings account in front of him. "Not enough," he says, closing the door further.

"Wait! There's more!" I pull extra cash out of my pocket and add it to my money fan. This is crazy. What if Mom and I need this money? What if Mom never comes back and I need the cash to get out of Scottsfield?

The door eases open. Mr. Jenkins unhooks the screen door and snatches the bills. He doesn't say *Thank you, good-bye,* or even *Sold.* He just shuts the door and turns the deadbolt.

I lean down and try to talk through the partially opened window. "Someone will be by in a few days to get him." Then Mr. Jenkins closes that, too.

When I get back home, Dad is washing his truck. He's kneeling in the bed of the pickup, scrubbing something with a brush. I try not to think about the missing shovel.

Don't be ridiculous, Sara! If Dad were trying to cover up evidence that he'd had a dead body in the truck, he would have done that last Tuesday, the day that Mom disappeared.

Right.

The day that I didn't come home until well after dinner. The day I found my dad alone in the dark, smoking.

To distract myself, I go inside and put on *The Winds of Change.* Julia, who's felt sick all week, finally takes a pregnancy test. Now surely she'll remember taking the same test once before and sharing the good news with her real husband. Instead there she is, jumping up and down next to Ramón. "We're going to have a baby!" she shouts.

Tomorrow is Tuesday, the day I've determined my mom will be back.

What if instead of coming to get me, Mom comes back to stay?

Decides to forgive Dad like she's always done before?

What will I do?

Will I stay here with her?

Or will I run?

Away. Far, far away.

Where Dad can never find me.

CHAPTER 12

Tuesday

Z ach and I have lunch at the Dairy Dream again on Tuesday. Without Alex.

"You want to sit here?" Zach asks, pointing to our usual table.

"It looks like there's something sticky on that one," I say. Actually, I just don't want to sit on that picnic bench without Alex.

"Is it my imagination or is Mrs. Hamilton glaring at us? Maybe we should buy something." Zach looks behind us, as if to see if there was anyone else she could be giving the evil eye to.

"She's just mad at me on account of Jessica's nose," I say weakly.

"Huh?" Zach furrows his brow.

"Turns out Jessica was supposed to be in some beauty pageant the day that I hit her with a volleyball. Apparently her nose swelled all up, got all red and puffy. She didn't win."

"I don't think that's the only reason she didn't win."

"Zach—"

"I know, I know. But it's the truth. Don't you have to be nice to win one of those pageants?"

"Moving on." I pull out the ham sandwiches I packed and hand one to Zach. "You know how my dad tends to put things back where they belong?"

"Wow. That's an understatement."

"Well, I was in the barn last night and I noticed that the shovel is missing."

"Missing? What do you mean, missing?"

"Missing. As in, not there."

"Okay, so?" Zach takes a bite of sandwich.

"Well, you don't think it means anything, do you?"

"Like what?" he asks, looking at me weird.

I can't help but think that Alex would have caught on to what I meant. But then again, Zach doesn't read Stephen King.

"You don't think my dad could have—You don't think he would have used the shovel to—You don't think he buried my mom somewhere, do you?" I pick at my sandwich, unable to eat.

Zach stops chewing. "Wow."

"Can you stop saying 'wow'? I mean, you don't really think so, do you? My mom is getting things set up for us somewhere, right?"

"Probably. I mean, maybe. I mean, we'd probably better check the field and the woods behind your house. Just in case." Zach takes another bite, then wraps up the rest of his sandwich and gets up from the picnic table.

Zach was supposed to be calming me down. Telling me that this was just crazy talk. Seeing him so agitated was making me feel like I had rocks in my stomach. I stand up quickly, banging my knee on the table, and throw my sandwich away without having eaten a single bite.

It's easy enough to skip afternoon classes. I've done it so much lately that I'm becoming a pro. We simply walk from the Dairy Dream to the parking lot and get into Zach's car. No one stops us or questions us. I guess it helps that Scottsfield's not big enough to have a parking-lot attendant or security guard.

"Park on the grass, next to the camper," I say when we get to my house. "Just in case Jack drives by the place and reports back to my dad."

Ever since my brother killed himself, Jack had increased his patrols past our house and reported anything suspicious back to Dad. A car in front of the house during school hours would definitely qualify as suspicious.

I slam the car door and look out at the hay fields dancing in the wind. "So what's the plan?" I ask.

"Why don't you start here and walk straight back. I'll go over that way about twenty feet and do the same. When we get to the end, we can move over and head back this way."

It feels good to have someone else making the decisions, even though I know I could have figured that out for myself. I put my arms in front of me as if I'm swimming, make a part in the hay, and step through. I try to walk as carefully as I can so my dad won't see any sign that we've been trampling through the field.

"How are you doing?" Zach calls.

"Okay, I guess."

What I really want to do is to throw myself on the ground and scream.

We find nothing, which is good news, I guess. No sign that anyone's been dragged, dumped, or buried. But there's still the woods, and the field in front of the house.

"The front field is too exposed," says Zach. "No one in his right mind would . . ." Zach's voice trails off.

Yeah, right. Still, I have to agree with Zach that we should concentrate on the woods. They belong to the farmer behind us, but they might as well belong to nobody, because as far as I know, no one ever sets foot in them.

As I enter the woods, a knot forms in my stomach. The tall trees, some starting to change colors, block the sunlight, lending a chill to the air. The wind picks up and the sound of leaves rustling reminds me of a fast-moving river. The tops of the trees creak, as if one might fall over at any minute. I duck involuntarily. Weaving this way and that, I try to find a clear route. Twigs and small branches slap my face. I turn back around, trying to make sure that I'm heading in as straight a line as possible, but I can no longer see our house or anything outside of the woods. I shiver as I imagine Dad carrying my mom through the woods and setting her down in front of the maple tree before me, confident that no one can see what he's doing.

I trip. I scream and clench my eyes shut, certain I've stumbled over Mom's leg. I can hear Zach's shoes crunching twigs and dried leaves as he runs to me. When I feel his hand on my shoulder, I dare to open my eyes. It's only a root.

Zach gives me a hug and we keep going, but this time he stays closer. We get to the marshy part and uneasiness trickles through my veins. The muck and water cover my ankles. With each step there's no way of knowing what I'll put my foot down on. Unlike the field in front of the house, this is the perfect place to hide a body. I start to shake. So much so that Zach notices.

"You don't have to do this," he says. "You can wait at the edge and I can do it. Or we can call the police."

"No. I can do this." If I call the police, Jack Reynolds and his crew will come busting back into our lives, Dad will convince them that my mom is on an extended vacation, and I'll be left alone with my dad who will know that I know.

The muck clings to my shoes. Every time I lift my foot it sounds like a sock stuck in the tube of the vacuum cleaner. Filthy water splashes my jeans and my shirt. I break a cattail in half and scatter the white fluffy filling in the water to distract myself from the real reason I'm here. Ten steps. Another cattail. Repeat. Twenty-seven cattails later and we've made it through the marsh.

"It's almost five," Zach says. "I better get out of here before your dad shows up." He extends his hand and we trudge back to the house together.

We go in through the garage and take a few careful steps to the laundry room. "Crap. I think these shoes are ruined. Yours too." I pry off my shoes and socks. "Hold on a sec," I say. "I'll get us some dry clothes."

In my room, I put on a new pair of jeans and grab some gray sweats for Zach. In the kitchen I get a jumbo garbage bag for our dirty stuff. I toss Zach the sweats. "What shoe size are you?"

"Eleven."

Close enough. Matt was a twelve. I go to Matt's room and fling open the door. "Hey, Matt, mind if Zach borrows your tennis shoes?" I say to the air. "I'm going to grab a pair of socks, too."

Zach must know the shoes are Matt's, but he doesn't say anything.

"Just let me stash this bag somewhere and I'll walk you out." The bag stinks. I stuff it in the back corner of my closet.

When I get back to the laundry room, Zach is wiping the floor with a towel. "Thanks," I say.

Five ten. My heart starts to beat faster. I take one last look to make sure that everything is the way it was this morning.

"You better get out of here," I say.

As we walk to his car, I look over at Zach, in my too-small sweats and Matt's too-big shoes. And for once, I just see Zach. Not my brother. Not my brother's best friend. My friend. "Thanks for doing this with me," I say.

"Of course," says Zach. "You know, I'm not sure you should be staying here. Maybe you should go stay with your grandparents. Or I can ask my parents—"

If Zach knew about the whole "let me force you to smoke a cigarette" incident, he'd be even less sure. "I'll be fine," I say. I close his car door and wave. Then I jog inside to start dinner.

* * *

The first thing Dad says when he gets home is "Who made those tire tracks out by the barn?"

My fingers and toes throb. Do I say something like, "Lauren came over to work on history"? I really want to blame it on he-who-refused-to-take-a-police-report Jack Reynolds, but that would buy me fifteen minutes at the most, before Dad un-verified it. The seconds tick by on the cuckoo clock. *Ticktock, ticktock, ticktock.* "What tracks?" I say, approximately six seconds too late.

"Don't play games with me."

I expect a slap, or perhaps a shove. Instead Dad grabs my wrist and drags me after him. Like a high-speed train, we whip through the house and out the front door. When a train is going fast enough, all you see are flashes of scenery. The same thing is happening to me, only the scenes that fly past are only in my mind. Me and Matt at the zoo, watching Matt's favorite animals—the monkeys. Us at home, making monkey faces at each other. Matt and I playing Uno at the kitchen table (Dad safely at work, so there's no chance he'll yell at us for playing something with Spanish in the title). Then we're in the auditorium at school. Matt is onstage and I'm in the audience, laughing out loud at a line he's just delivered.

By the time we reach the barn, my little mind-movie is over. It ends where it always does: with Matt dead on the dining room floor. I want so badly for it to start over, even though I know it will always end the same.

Dad pushes me to my knees, then, clutching the back of my neck, he propels my face toward the flattened grass, as if I'm a dog who's just messed in the living room. "These tire tracks."

"I don't know anything about them."

"Like hell you don't!" He pushes hard and quick, and my face slams into the grass. The pain in my nose forces tears to my eyes. I lick my lips to see if they're bleeding and end up tasting a paste of dirt and blood.

"I'm going to ask you one more time. Who made these tire tracks?"

I don't hesitate this time. *Whatever you do, don't say Zach. Don't say Zach. Don't say Zach.* I'm not getting Zach any more mixed-up in this mess than he already is. "I really don't know."

Dad kicks me in the shin. The knee. The stomach. I seal my face with my arms, making it hard to breathe, and squeeze my eyes shut. This time the flashes are all of my mom—her head slammed into the wall, the frying pan thrown at her feet, the broken arm, the hand shattered by the car door. *If you had said something, if you had done something, Sara, this wouldn't be happening now. You deserve this.* A boot strikes my back and I whimper. Then the footsteps crunch away and it's quiet except for a fly buzzing overhead.

The truck rumbles to life. I expect it to take off and fade away. Instead it roars louder as it closes in on me. He's going to run me over!

I scramble to my feet. It's like I'm stuck in a dream with the horn of a train blaring at me to get out of the way, only I can't move because, of course, it's only a dream and your legs don't work when you're stuck inside a dream. But this isn't a dream because there's no horn blasting, no conductor wanting me to move, only the roar of the truck that doesn't care what it flattens.

Run! Run! Run! Far away! Don't stop! Thump!

My eyes tell my leg about the tree stump, but only after it's too late. The air gets sucked out of my lungs as I slam into the ground. I don't know if I can get up again. I wish I had time to say good-bye to Zach. To Alex.

Alex! God, how I wish I were back in history class. That I'd fallen asleep reading Stephen King and that Alex was tapping my shoulder. No, take that back—kissing my ear. Pitching paper airplanes at me. Whatever. Doing *anything* so I can just wake up! Goddamn it, why can't I just wake up?

Brakes shriek. The truck idles a few feet from my head. I can feel its hot breath panting down on my face. Then I hear the angry sound of the gear shift being slammed some way it doesn't want to go, and the hot breath is gone. The truck careens backward as recklessly as it had sped forward, cutting paths in the field. Forward again. Only this time it rumbles down the driveway and out onto the road.

I look up at the sky. The clouds float serenely by, as if nothing has changed. Just like at school, where everyone still worries about the grade they got on their math test and if a certain shirt makes them look fat. It's nearly impossible to watch everything and everyone act the same when for me, the whole world has changed.

Mom, how could you leave me?

CHAPTER 13

Wednesday

Sara?"

I look up from the book I'm not reading. Mrs. Monroe is standing by the door. She waves me over. "You need to go down to the assistant principal's office."

Me? I'm never in trouble. It has to be—

My heart starts to pound. *Please, please let it be!* If I think it hard enough, maybe it will be true.

All of that imagining that my dad has somehow killed my mom is just that, just my imagination—the end result of reading too much horror and watching too much of *The Winds of Change*. Mom is here, almost like we planned.

Altman's calling you down because you've been missing classes, Sara. That's it. Classes. Your mom isn't here. It's just the classes. All anyone around here cares about are classes.

"No! It's her!" From the way everyone is looking at me, I might have said that out loud. I throw down my English book and pick up my backpack. It *is* my mom. It has to be. I grind my teeth together.

Mrs. Monroe tries to pat me on the shoulder as I whisk by her. "I'm sure it's nothing."

I walk quickly down the hall, past the new yellow lockers installed just this year and assigned to seniors only. Then I turn the corner to the gray-locker hallway. There's Alex, bent over the drinking fountain, sucking down half of Scottsfield's water supply. He isn't in class. What a surprise. I wonder what proportion of time Alex is in class versus the time he spends in the halls.

I hesitate, like when a squirrel runs out in front of your car and you know you're going to hit it. If my mom is here, I have to hurry! I can't stop to talk in the hallway. But also, if my mom is here, I'll never see Alex again.

It turns out I don't have to make a decision. As soon as Alex looks at me, all my resolve melts.

"Hey, Sara," he says.

"Hi." *Breathe!*

He examines his shoes.

Before I can think, I run to him. If I'm going, I can't just leave things the way they are. I reach up and put my hands on top of his two adorable ears and tug his face down to mine. *God, I love you, Alex Maloy. Too bad I can't stay.* Then I kiss him. I mean I *really* kiss him.

"Wow." He wears a happy, goofy grin.

"So when are you going to start going to class?"

His smile fades.

Way to spoil the moment, Sara.

"The truth?"

"Yeah, the truth would be good."

"I don't know. Ever since Jimmy got sent to Afghanistan—"

"Wait—your brother's in Afghanistan?" Jimmy graduated from Scottsfield two years ago.

Alex kicks a corner of one of the lockers. "School, classes, grades—it all kind of seems unimportant—when your brother might be—" He shakes his head.

"You know your brother would want you to be successful, even if he—" *And your brother, Sara, would want you to stop pretending his best friend is really him. He'd want you to stop blaming yourself for what he did.*

"Shit, it's Altman." Alex grabs my arm and pulls me around the corner. "Go to class. I'll run interference."

"No, it's okay. I got called down to his office. *You* go to class and *I'll* run interference."

Alex frowns. "I hadn't really planned on going back to class." He leans down and places another soft kiss on my lips. "But for you, I'll go." He smiles again and waves as he jogs backward down the hall.

I smile and wave back. "Good-bye, Alex," I whisper. As much as I'm praying to get my mom back, I wish I could stay so I could see his face every day. I touch my fingers to my lips, remembering kissing and being kissed. As Alex disappears around one corner, Altman rounds the other.

"There you are, Sara. Hurry up; I've been waiting for you." He spins back around and heads toward his office.

I've *been waiting for you? Not, Your* mom's *been waiting for you?*

I freeze and all my happiness escapes out the tips of my toes. Then I shake my head. *Pull yourself together, Sara. She's there. She has to be there.*

I jog the rest of the way to Altman's office. I'm out of breath when I arrive—I'm not sure if it's from the jogging, from kissing Alex, or from the fear Mom won't be there. I scan the office: Altman sits at his desk with a pile of magazines, sipping coffee from a mug that says SHOW YOU CARE. He gestures toward a wooden chair. No Mom. She must be getting a copy of my records from the guidance office for our move.

I don't have time to sit, but I do anyhow, perched on the end of the seat like we're supposed to do in band. "Yes?" I ask, wondering what story my mom made up to explain why I'm leaving.

"How are your classes going, Sara?"

"My classes? Fine." *What is this shit? Who cares about my classes?*

"How about math?"

Is he going to tell me that I should try an easier math class at my next school? "Okay, I guess."

"It has come to my attention that you've missed three math classes in the past week. Chemistry, too."

She isn't here. I slump down into the chair.

"Yeah, I guess so."

"You guess so?" He lifts his eyebrows.

"Yeah, I missed them. I had a dentist appointment."

"All three days?"

"Orthodontist, actually. I'm getting braces."

"Really? Your teeth don't look crooked to me."

"Thanks."

"As of right now, those absences are listed as unexcused."

"Really? My mom didn't call? She said she was going to."

"No. No, she didn't." Altman grits his teeth. "And there is also the matter of your not signing out before you left."

"Signing out? Did I forget to do that? It's been ages since I've had an appointment. Sorry about that." I look around the office. Football calendar. Potted tree—what guy has a potted tree in his office? I wonder if it's fake.

"This is a very serious matter, young lady."

"I'll have my mom call you right away." *If I can find her. Of course, if I do, I'm never coming back here so it won't really matter.* My jaw shakes a little as I speak. I go back to examining the room to keep myself from crying. There's a picture of a sailboat above the potted plant. Lots of light blue and pastel colors. I stare at it and imagine I'm on the boat, drifting.

"I'm afraid I'm going to have to have one of your parents come in."

As long as it's not my dad. "Sure. I'll have my mom stop in tomorrow." During the last week I've told so many lies, I don't even bother trying to keep track of them anymore.

"I'll call and set it up with her."

Whatever you do, don't call my dad. I start to twirl my ponytail.

"Would you like me to give you her cell phone number?" I try to calm myself by pretending that maybe when Mom sees the school calling, she'll know something is seriously wrong and she'll answer. Then she'll come pick me up and take me away with her.

"That's okay. It's here on your emergency contact form." He taps a manila folder on his desk. It looks pretty thin. That's good, I guess. I've never had any progress reports sent home, detentions for tardies, or referrals for "inappropriate behavior."

"Sara, is anything wrong?"

Twist, twist. I'm twirling my hair with such force that I yank out a few strands.

I think about my mom not answering her phone. My dad and his driving. Alex and piano benches, Nick Russell's basement, and lying about the Chicken Broil. Zach and me breaking into my dad's store, trekking through the muck in the woods, and the hot breath of a truck.

"Wrong?" I try to look perky and carefree. "No, nothing's wrong." I stand up, like this is a business meeting with a client and I need to get back to the office. "Well, then, I guess I'll be getting back to class. If we're done here, that is."

Altman stays seated. His hands are poised in a triangular shape in front of his lips, as if he is trying to think of something good and counselor-like to say.

"Yes, we're done here," he says, picking up a pad of yellow passes and scrawling my name and something that I assume is supposed to pass for his signature. He holds the pen over the blank for "time," looks directly at me for several seconds, and then fills it in. Then he rips the pass off the pack, hands it to me, and leans back in his seat.

I wonder if Altman is going to call Zach in next, since we've both missed those periods. I don't know what Zach will tell his mom about the classes he's missed, but I'm sure that he won't mention me unless he has to. Funny that Altman didn't say anything about Zach. Surely he realized that we were gone at most of the same times. Or maybe not. Altman never struck me as the observant type. Besides, I've missed more classes than Zach. And Alex? Alex has missed so many classes that there's no way Altman would be connecting those dots.

The bell rings just as I'm leaving, so I head to history. As I walk through the door everything goes dark.

"Get your hands off my eyes, Alex," I say. *If we weren't in the middle of history class I'd tell you a better place to put them.*

"How'd you know it was me? I guess I'll have to give you your surprise with your eyes open."

"Surprise?"

Alex unzips his backpack and tosses a package of Ritz Bits at me.

"Thanks," I say, smiling. *Where have you been my whole life, Alex Maloy?* "Now it's my turn to ask—how did you know?"

"Oh, I have my sources. Okay, one source. Name of Zach."

I pop open the bag. "Want some?"

"Does Robertson hate my guts? Of course I want some."

Instead of taking the Ritz Bits out of my hand, Alex simply holds my hand, with the Ritz Bits snuggled between us.

"Maloy!" Robertson shouts.

Alex drops my hand. The Ritz Bits fall to the ground.

"Go see Mr. Altman."

"For hand-holding?"

"Not for hand-holding." Robertson rolls his eyes and sighs. "For whatever other trouble you've gotten yourself into."

"Oh, that. Well, as long as I'm already in trouble—" Alex leans over and kisses me. And again. And—

The class goes wild.

"Out!"

I take my seat, completely but happily embarrassed, and Robertson tries to start his lecture. You can barely hear him over all the giggling and catcalling still going on. I don't even bother trying. I'm too busy thinking of Alex, of kissing him, and him being worried about his brother. Kicking the locker. The *locker*. I finally remember where I've seen the name "Carter"—Carter Mini Storage. We'd passed it a few times when Dad was teaching Matt how to drive a stick shift on some backroads by the hardware store. Dad had said, "What the hell do people need storage units for? If you don't need the shit, throw it out!"

Did Dad rent a storage unit? He even throws out things he doesn't think other people need (such as my stuffed dog). The only unused stuff he keeps around is in Matt's room, and lately it seems that's because he thinks Matt still uses it.

I take my purse out of my backpack and start digging around for that scrap of paper. First I check the little inner zipper compartment used to hide things you don't want people to see when you open your purse. As far as I can tell, without pulling everything out of the pocket, it isn't there. Next I flip through a mess of old receipts and hall passes stuffed in the main part of my purse. *Where is that piece of paper?* I do not want to have to break into the hardware store again. I mean, I guess it's not really breaking in when you have the key, but all the same, the idea scares the hell out of me. Finally I pull out my wallet and check by the dollar bills.

"Sara, this is not personal-organization time," says Mr. Robertson. "Pay attention please."

It never ceases to amaze me how teachers manage to say "please" when what they really mean is "or I'll break your neck."

"Okay," I say, pulling out the stack of random things I had filed in my wallet where you're supposed to keep credit cards, if you have any.

I find the sticky note about halfway through the stack. Carter. Three, six, two, nine, four, seven. I put the other cards back in my wallet and shove it back in my purse. I pick up my pencil and write random numbers on my worksheet while I silently count to ten. Keeping the pencil as a prop in my right hand and my eyes on the textbook, I slide my cell phone out of my jeans pocket and send a text message to Zach:

NEED YOUR CAR NOW. BACK DOOR BY CHOIR RM. URGENT.

"Sara, you know that cell phones aren't allowed in class. Hand it over."

Somehow Robertson is standing next to my desk, but I don't think he saw my message to Zach before I sent it. He holds out his hand.

"It's my mom. She wants me to call her. I told her I'm in class and I'll call her at lunch. I'll put it away."

"Sorry, you know the rules. Hand it over."

I shove the phone in my pocket. There's no way I'm going to hand over the one way my mom can contact me.

"I can't." I say simply.

"Sara, I'll have to write you a referral if you don't turn it in. You can get the phone back at the end of the day."

"I understand," I say. "I'll save you the bother. I'll just go to Mr. Altman's office myself." *Had I actually said that?* Robertson looks startled.

I stand up, grab my backpack, and move quickly to the door. On my way, I crush the Ritz Bits that Alex and I dropped. I hope that Zach got my message.

"Sara, get back here!"

I speed up and start to run down the hall. *Please let Zach be there. Please, God.* I don't often talk to God—I guess you can say I'm holding a grudge about Matt—but I really hope he's listening.

I fly past the science rooms, the library, and the gym. When I get to the back door, Zach is there. He hands me his keys.

"Thanks," I say. "Gotta go. I think Robertson might send Altman after me." I push open the door and keep running. When I get to the parking lot, I pause to look for Zach's car.

Zach grabs my hand. "It's this way," he says. "I'm coming with you."

"No, I'll be okay," I say. "You've already missed enough school because of me."

"Doesn't matter," he says.

I don't have time for arguing. With each second that passes, I imagine Altman hurrying to the back door, getting closer and closer to catching me.

"You drive, then," I say, tossing him the keys.

Zach jumps in the car and starts the engine. He backs up while still pulling on his seat belt.

"Turn right out of the parking lot and don't speed," I say. "The last thing we need is to get stopped."

"Where are we going?"

"Carter Mini Storage. The numbers in my dad's office must be the combination for a unit there. My dad probably just has some old junk from the hardware store there, but . . ."

"Probably. But there's no harm in checking. Where is this place?"

"Outside of Brookton, somewhere off of Ridge Highway." I look up the address on my phone. "I remember going past it when Dad took Matt out to practice driving and I got stuck going along."

"I'm sure your dad was a very patient instructor," Zach says sarcastically.

"Yeah, right." I roll my eyes. Since my dad's truck is a stick shift and Matt wasn't used to it, he had jerked us forward every time he hit the gas. Dad made Matt stop and start a lot because we were on dirt roads with barely any traffic. Instead of getting better, Matt seemed to get worse every time. And so did Dad's yelling.

Zach and I pull up to a stop sign. I look down at the directions on my phone. "Turn right. It's over there," I say, pointing. Nestled between two cornfields, Carter Mini Storage consists of a farmhouse with a bunch of metal buildings behind it. Zach pulls in and turns off the engine. I wipe the sweat from my hands on my jeans. "So what do you think? We just go to the front door?"

"Sounds good to me."

When we knock, I can hear a TV blaring on the other side. "It's open!"

The door sticks so I have to push kind of hard on it. A middle-aged woman sits barefoot on a couch. *Judge Judy* is on TV.

The woman's eyes remain focused on the TV. I clear my throat. "Excuse me, ma'am. My dad sent me over here to get something out of our storage unit, but I forgot what unit number he told me it is." My cheeks flush and I have to wipe the sweat off my hands once again. I expect her to say that she's going to have to call my dad to confirm, or that she's sorry, but she can't give out that sort of information. Instead she just sighs.

"Name?" The gravelly tone to her voice makes sense considering the cigarette in her hand.

"Ray Peters."

Without turning her head, she reaches behind her and grabs a Rolodex from the end table. She flips through it with one hand, then inhales deeply from her cigarette and blows out the smoke. She crushes the stub into a glass ashtray. "Number eleven," she says.

I nearly hyperventilate. "Okay, great, thanks a lot for your help."

The woman has already turned back to the TV.

Outside, Zach and I walk down the path between the storage units, and I feel like I'm trapped inside a movie. I see things but don't feel like I'm really there. Grass with weeds, dandelions. A toad hopping in front of us, going just fast enough that we don't step on him, but never veering off to the side and out of our way. Zach takes my hand. It feels cool and confident; mine is warm and clammy. We reach unit eleven and I give him the sticky note with the combination.

"You do it, please."

He twirls the lock, and it snaps open with a sharp, metallic *click*. Then he rolls the door up. Silver.

I hear a whimper and realize that it's coming from me. I grab on to Zach's shirt and bury my face in his side.

"This can't be right. It just can't be." My mother's car. I feel like I'm suffocating. Still holding on to Zach, I turn my face and look at the car again. Something about the look of it bothers me.

The car sparkles as if it's just been cleaned at the carwash. Which doesn't make sense because my mom is afraid of the car wash, just like me. She's afraid of putting the wheel in the wrong spot, of having the car in the wrong gear, of getting trapped inside and no one noticing. Matt always did it for her. It was one of his chores—to either wash the car at home with the hose or take it to the car wash in Brookton. He usually took it to the car wash, partly because he was lazy and partly because he wanted to get out of the house, I suppose. After he died, I took over the car washing. And this isn't how I'd left it. Usually I wash the car on weekends, but I'd never gotten around to it last weekend. The car had been so dirty I had been afraid my dad would yell at me about it.

I put my face to the window and peer into the front seat. It looks the same as always, only cleaner. I reach for the handle.

"We probably shouldn't touch anything," says Zach. He takes

the end of his shirt and opens the driver's-side door. On the floor of the passenger seat is my mother's phone.

Zach opens the trunk as I look in the backseat. "There's a suitcase here," he says. I walk to the back of the car. It's the same suitcase that my mom had packed for our escape.

This time I don't try to dream up any explanations, any hopeful stories to explain all of this away. My mom is dead. My dad killed her.

All I want to do is go home. To my mom. Who isn't there and never will be.

Zach pulls out his cell phone. "I'm calling the police."

I shake my head. My mind is full of voices. Mom's. Dad's. Matt's, even. "Did you—did you see any—did you see any blood here?"

"No, but that doesn't mean . . ."

"When Dad talks to Jack—" His wolf eyes glint in my mind.

"I know. He might try to convince the police that your mom left on her own."

"Take me home, Zach. I need to get some things."

"Sara—"

"Please, Zach. Just please take me home."

CHAPTER 14

Wednesday

What if your dad's home?" Zach asks, unbuckling his seat belt.

"He's not. It's only twelve thirty. He doesn't believe in leaving work early, even when he's sick." Just to be sure, once we're out of the car, I peer into the garage. No truck. Safe, for the moment.

Zach takes my hand and we go inside. "I just want to get a few things," I say. *Mainly my mom's necklace. And Sam—as stupid and messed up as that is.* "Come with me?" I ask, gripping his hand a little tighter.

"Of course," says Zach. We cross through the living room, where something smells fruity. An orange. "Do you smell that?" I ask Zach.

He nods.

I look around. It isn't like my dad to leave out a plate or a peel after a snack. Nothing. Then I freeze.

Dad is sitting at the dining room table, eating orange slices. My heart beats furiously. No one goes into the dining room. It's off-limits because of Matt. We all know that. We all respect the unspoken rule. Yet there he is, sitting and eating as if nothing has changed.

Every instinct tells me to run. Instead I approach the dining room, but I don't go in. Zach stands next to me.

"Your school called. Said you had skipped out. Again," Dad says nonchalantly.

"We found Mom's car," I say accusingly.

My dad pushes his chair back and stands up, walking toward me with measured steps.

Zach makes a fist.

A glint of silver in Dad's hand. Just seeing it starts my whole body trembling. A gun.

The gun Matt used to kill himself.

Zach hesitates. My dad does not. He smacks the gun against Zach's head, and Zach crumples to the floor.

I swing my backpack at Dad. He blocks it, grabbing my wrist and forcing me to my knees next to Zach.

Zach's body is still, his face expressionless, his skin smooth and flawless. He looks how I wished my brother would have looked when he died. Serene. Peaceful. Beautiful.

I kiss the tops of his eyelids, like I had wanted to do to Matt. *Please, God, let him still be alive.* I press my face against his and feel his soft, cool cheek. His warm breath tickles my ear. *Thank you, God.*

Dad yanks me to my feet. My head hits the wall and a picture frame falls to the floor and cracks. "Go pack his bag," he says. "Now that Matt doesn't have play rehearsal anymore we can finally go on vacation." He gestures toward Matt's room.

"We need to call an ambulance." I can barely hear my own voice over the roaring in my ears.

"He'll be fine."

Dad waves me along with the gun and follows me into Matt's room.

This can't be happening. This is my dad, the same dad who gave me Sam. Who used to call me "angel," who took me biking, fishing, train-watching, horseback riding, and to see the Statue of Liberty.

"Pack."

Why hadn't I left the day my mom didn't show up at the Dairy Dream? I kept believing she was alive long after it made any sense. *I'm sorry, Zach. Sorry for getting you into this mess.*

Dad sits on Matt's bed, patiently watching me. *Who is this person?*

I open Matt's dresser drawers. They're all neatly organized—too organized. I want to cry, but instead I choose the same kind of stuff I'd packed for myself last Monday night: underwear, socks, jeans, a few T-shirts, and a sweatshirt for good measure. Only one, because *wherever we're going, whatever we're doing, it can't last for very long.*

Then I go into my bathroom, the one Matt and I used to share, and I find a new toothbrush. There's one in the drawer that Mom had bought before Matt died. It's red. Matt's color.

I take Matt's duffel into the living room and set it down.

"Go ahead, pack yours, too," my dad says encouragingly. He seems to be in a great mood, despite the gun in his hand. He follows me into my room.

I'd already repacked most of my duffel in preparation for Mom's return. I slide it out from under the bed and toss in the rest on autopilot. Including Sam. Dad doesn't seem to remember that Sam is supposed to be in a Dumpster. I reach for a pen on my desk.

"Nope. This is a no-homework vacation."

"Great. Then I'll take a pen for crossword puzzles. What else should I bring? Where are we going?"

Dad laughs and shakes his head, as if I've just told him the world's best joke.

"You hate crosswords." Then his face loses its color and he stops laughing. Matt was the one who liked crosswords.

"I can bring it along for—"

"I said no!"

"Then I'll just bring something to read."

My dad nods, jaw clenched, as I tear out a page from *Soap Opera Digest* and slip it into Alex's Stephen King book.

Dad escorts me to the living room and nods for me to pick up Matt's—Zach's—bag too. "Ladies first."

With a bag over each arm and the Stephen King book in one hand, I cross through the kitchen. I sway to the left, pretending my balance is off, and drop one of the bags. I lurch toward the phone, knocking a chair over on the way. Then I grab the receiver and hit talk. My dad doesn't try to stop me.

No dial tone.

Dad looks at me like when I was five and I'd say, "Can I have another cookie, please?" And he'd say, "There aren't any more." I'd check anyhow. He'd let me, and he wouldn't get mad. His eyes would just say, *See? I told you,* when I saw the cookie jar was empty.

And, like when I was five, Dad now says, "Come on, Sara. Let's get going."

I pick up the bag and take long, quick steps—fast enough to make it outside a few seconds before my dad, but not so fast that it looks as if I'm trying to run away.

Outside, the birds sing and the sun shines, and the car going by at the end of our quarter-mile-long driveway seems as far away from me and my voice as stars in the night sky.

I toss Alex's book across the lawn like a Frisbee. I'm sure that once he learns that I walked out on Robertson's class and never came back, he'll come by the house to try to find out what happened. Beyond that, I can only hope he'll find the book he loaned me and realize that something's wrong. That he'll notice the *Soap Opera Digest* page and remember Zach teasing me about keeping my magazines in pristine condition. Hopefully he doesn't think I'm incredibly careless or that I've taken to reading on the front lawn. But even if he figures out something is wrong, how will Alex know where to find me when I don't even know, myself?

Although in my mind it seems about as discreet as a billboard, Dad doesn't notice the abandoned book. He simply gestures toward the camper, parked as it always is next to the barn. As we pass the side door of the barn, I see that Dad's parked his truck inside it.

Brilliant, Sara. You checked the garage but not the barn. In my defense, Dad never parks in the barn. Which means he planned all of this and knew I wasn't going to go with him willingly.

I hesitate at the stairs to the camper. This is absurd. *Run, Sara, run! This is your last chance!* But where do I run? We're in the middle of a twenty-acre field and our only neighbor won't even open the door for me.

My dad is behind me. He prods me forward with the gun and my heart nearly stops beating. I force my feet up the steps and into the camper. It smells of tuna fish and Cheerios, my dad's favorite camping foods. Now that I'm inside, will I ever come back out?

My dad takes the duffel bags and finds a place for them, then pushes me onto the bench next to the table. The walls seem to close in and the space becomes even smaller than I remembered it. *I have to get out!* There has to be something I can use to smash the window.

Dad opens a drawer calmly and deliberately and pulls something out. Handcuffs. He tosses them to me. "Put one on."

Seriously?

He points the gun at me. What if I refuse? Will he really shoot me? He must have shot Mom. Which means he'll shoot me and Zach. If not now, then later. Maybe I should just let it be now.

I hesitate, but only for a moment. As much as I hate my life right now, I don't want it to end. Even if I can see Matt. And Mom. I click a handcuff onto one wrist.

"Sit on the floor."

I don't want to. I want to stay on the bench where I can try to pretend that things are normal. I don't want to sit on the floor where I won't even be able to see where we're going.

"Move, Sara!" my dad barks.

I slide to the floor.

"Hands behind your back." It sounds so absurd that I want to laugh and say, *Geez, Dad, you've been watching too much* Law & Order. Although, in Dad's case, I guess he had just *lived* too much *Law & Order.*

Dad cuffs my hands together around the giant table leg, which is attached to the floor of the camper. He has to set down the gun to do it. *This is my chance!*

I try to stand up and I scream, even though I know the rest of the world is too far away to hear me.

I'm not fast enough. The handcuffs are secured. I keep screaming. My dad picks up the gun again and points it at me. He looks angrier, like the next time he points the gun at me he's going to use it. He's going to pull the trigger.

I stop screaming. He picks up a roll of duct tape, cuts off a strip, and comes toward me. My heart beats wildly.

"Hold still," he says, and covers my mouth with the strip.

Dad leaves and a few minutes later comes back carrying Zach. He props him up and handcuffs him to the table leg too. "I was hoping I wouldn't need these." He ruffles Zach's hair.

I like to imagine that Zach is my brother, too. At least *I* know it's just pretend.

I want to cry.

Dad takes another strip of duct tape and covers Zach's mouth, even though he's still unconscious. Then Dad gets out a plastic tablecloth that my mom always clips onto picnic tables. He shakes it over the table so that it drapes down and covers us, and even uses the plastic clips to hold it in place. My world is darker still.

Dad's shoes squeak on the steps of the camper and then the back door slams. The camper shifts ever so slightly as Dad gets in the front. He closes the door, turns on the engine, and starts to whistle.

The camper bumps and rattles and turns corners. Each bump spills a tear that I'm trying to will back into my eyes. I know if I really let myself cry I won't be able to stop. I feel like I'm going to be carsick. *Please don't let me throw up.* The handcuffs dig into my wrists, and I ache all over.

Then I hear the most beautiful sound: a siren! *Please let it be for us.*

The camper slows. I feel us veer to the side, and the slight drop as we edge onto the shoulder. We stop. There's a slight shake as a vehicle whooshes past us. Then we start rolling again.

I don't remember anything in my *Worst-Case Scenario* guidebook about escaping handcuffs. I curse myself for not having bought the second book in the series. I'm on my own.

Mom, I'm so scared. I really thought you were coming back. I miss you.

You and Matt have to help me figure out how to get Zach away from here. He's been so good to us. We have to make it up to him.

I close my eyes and try to think about something else. I imagine that Alex is next to me, rubbing my shoulders. What time is it? School will surely be over soon. I wonder what Alex thought when he got back to history and I wasn't there. Did he go to the Dairy Dream? What did he think when I wasn't at the Dairy Dream, when I wasn't in math? Or maybe he skipped math. Would he try to find me? I think about kissing him before he got sent to Altman's office.

The ride gets more and more bumpy, and after a while, I don't even hear the whoosh of other passing cars. We're going a lot slower, but the potholes are horrific and I keep whacking my head on the top of the table. We've made so many turns that there's no way I could have kept track of how to get home.

Finally, we stop. The engine noise fades into a bubbling sound. We must be near a river. My stomach bottoms out as I process what that means. *Is Dad going to drown us? Is that what he did to my mom?* Between that thought and the duct tape over my mouth it becomes doubly hard to breathe.

Calm down, Sara! Think this through! What did Dad *say* when he told me to pack the bags? *"Now that Matt doesn't have play rehearsal, we can finally go on vacation."*

Vacation. It's starting to make sense. What if this isn't just any river? What if it's the Au Sable? Dad said *vacation.* What if he brought us back to Ramona's Retreat, where we spent all those summers? We stopped going there after Matt died, but Dad has been acting as if Zach is Matt and Matt is still alive.

The back door opens, Dad pulls back the tablecloth, and I see that I'm right. There's the wooden eagle statue mounted on a stump that's been here as long as I can remember. We're at Ramona's Retreat.

The next-closest cabin isn't within screaming distance, which I'm sure is why Dad pulls the duct tape off my mouth. My lips sting and I cry out in pain. Zach is starting to come to and Dad rips his duct tape off too.

Dad opens a drawer, takes out a key, and unlocks my left hand-cuff. Once he takes it off I realize how tight it had been and I rub my wrist.

"Move," Dad says, dropping the key back into the drawer. He gestures toward the door with the gun.

The air smells woodsy and is cool by the river. It's hard to look at the cabin. If I focus on the front window, I see Matt chasing Mom with a water gun. If I look toward the river, I see Matt filling up a bucket of water to dump on me. If I look up, Matt's sitting in a tree, smiling down at me. But I know that I've gone completely mad, just like my dad, when I walk inside the cabin.

"Mom!"

My mom sits in a kitchen chair, duct tape over her mouth, cov-ered with a blanket. I start to cry. Whatever madness this is, I don't want to get better.

I run to her and throw my arms around her. Her face is red and bruised. I touch the tears running down her cheeks, and reassure myself that she's real.

For a moment, I feel a rush of joy. *She's alive! My mom's alive!*

Dad peels the duct tape from her mouth. I hug her again but she isn't hugging me back because she's handcuffed to the chair. Her feet are tied at a horrible angle, so she can't use them to stand. The joy I felt just moments ago is sucked right out of me. My mom is alive, but after this will she ever be the same? And if she's been a prisoner here all week, how will any of us escape?

Dad yanks me away to the opposite side of the kitchen. He attaches my other handcuff to the refrigerator door. Then he straightens the towel on the oven door and lines up three tuna cans along the back of the counter. So this is what happened to the fifty dollars' worth of groceries on the credit card statement.

"I'll just go get Matt," my dad says, all cheery. Mom's face jerks as if she's been slapped.

"He thinks Zach is Matt," I say as soon as he's back outside.

"No, Sara. No, you can't be here," Mom says frantically. She's shaking and her words run together. "You've got to get away. I'm sorry that I waited so long. I'd hoped you had run away. And now Zach—I love you, baby."

"I love you too, Mom. It's not your fault. We'll find a way out of here." I try to mask the waver in my voice. The truth is, I'm utterly terrified and without a plan. I instinctively reach for my ponytail and turn it round and round. "Have you been alone here all this time?"

She shakes her head. "No, your dad's been here most of every day."

Dad, who's never late for work and never leaves early, has been coming *here*? I feel stupid as I realize that's the reason he had Bruce working extra hours.

I look around the kitchen. "Where's the phone?"

"Your dad cut the line, then he took the phone with him."

Just like he did at home.

Zach stumbles into the room. He looks up, sees my mom, and almost smiles. "Mrs.—"

"Matt!" I shout over him. "Mom was just asking about the field trip you went on today."

Zach's expression deflates. "Fine," he says. "The field trip was fine."

Dad pushes Zach into a kitchen chair and fastens his handcuffs through the rungs. Dad grabs a coil of rope from the kitchen counter. Zach kicks, but my dad grabs his foot and twists until Zach screams. Then he makes a few quick, tight knots, just like when he ties up the trash, and Zach's legs are as useless as my mom's. Dad: 3. Us: 0.

I try to stay calm by looking around the cabin for a weapon or a way out. I wonder if my dad went to the trouble of renting the cabin or whether he just broke in. Either way, since it isn't summer, it seems unlikely that anyone else will drop by to visit.

"All right, then, I'll make us some dinner." Dad usually does the cooking, if you can call it that, when we go camping.

Next to me in the kitchen, Dad opens a can of tuna, mixes it with some mayonnaise that he gets out of the refrigerator I'm attached to, and pops bread into the toaster. Then he puts a kettle on the stove for tea. When it's all ready, he brings our plates to the table.

Dad slides Mom's chair over to the table. Next to a pair of antlers, there's a hook on the wall. Dad grabs a small key from it. *A key to the handcuffs? He must have two copies, since he didn't hang anything there when he came in from the camper with Zach.* Dad frees a hand for Mom and Zach each to eat with. He moves me to a kitchen chair, only he doesn't tie my legs like everyone else's. I guess there are some advantages to being known as She Who Has No Voice When It Matters.

The tea is good. It always is when Dad makes it. I put my nose close to the cup to warm up. Then I take a sip—perfectly sweet.

The tuna sandwich is another story. It has the crunchy things in it that I hate. I want to pick them out, but I don't dare. So I bite and chew and swallow and try to drown the taste and the texture with the tea.

Dad's eyes are bright and shiny. Unlike most nights, he carries the conversation.

"So, Matt. Ready to do some canoeing soon?"

"Um. Yeah. Sure," Zach says as he eats his sandwich. Long pause. "Dad." The real Matt would have paused too, because Matt didn't like canoeing. For our last canoe trip, Dad woke us up at five a.m. with urgent shouts to get outside. I leaped out of bed and threw on my clothes, hands shaking as if the fire alarm had just gone off. Outside, Dad had all of our life jackets lined up on a log next to the river. I reluctantly slipped mine on. It reeked from being stuffed in a plastic bag while it was still wet.

"Matt, grab the cooler," Dad had said, stepping in the canoe.

"Get it yourself," Matt said, only Dad never heard because I pretended to swallow wrong and have a coughing fit. I picked up the cooler with one hand and grabbed Matt's sleeve with the other, dragging both to the canoe. Even though we'd been doing this for years, Matt and I still didn't paddle to Dad's satisfaction. Dad was always shouting, "Other side, Sara!"

Dad drops a plastic bowl on the table, startling me back to the present.

"Chips, anyone?" Dad asks. We all put on smiles and dutifully push our plates forward.

The gun lies on the counter next to the bag of chips, the barrel pointing straight at me. As my dad refills the chip bowl, I wonder what would happen if he bumped the gun off the counter. Would it go off? Would someone get hit?

As we eat, Dad prods us each in turn to talk about our day. Mom's reply, spoken in her fake-cheery voice, sounds rehearsed and strangely familiar. "Call volume was up today. We were running a special on the Autumn Splendor sets. I showed you one of the plates, right, Sara?"

"Uh, yeah, right," I say. No wonder it sounds familiar. That's the exact same thing she said the day before she disappeared.

I look at my Dad, wondering if he's caught on. Apparently not. He nods and smiles.

I get the feeling that Mom's been saying the same thing every night. Maybe because she'd figured out that it's safe. That there's nothing she'd said to make my dad upset.

"How was your day, Sara?"

I take a deep breath and repeat what I'd said last Monday night too.

"Fine, I guess. Rachel spilled hydrochloric acid on herself in chem and had to use the emergency shower."

On cue, Mom adds, "She's okay, I hope."

"Yeah, she's fine."

"Matt?"

We all look at Zach. The wild card. Would he say the right thing? Would he remember Matt's schedule? More important, would *Dad* remember Matt's schedule?

Don't mention Spanish class. Whatever you do, please don't mention Spanish class. Or the Dairy Dream. Or play rehearsal. Especially not play rehearsal.

"I, uh, had a test in math?"

Dad nods. "And?"

"And I did good. Uh, ninety-two."

Watch it, Zach! Matt would never have done that well.

"It's graded already?" Dad's voice sounds suspicious.

"Not everyone's. Just mine. I thought I'd done well, so I asked if she could grade it for me after school." He's starting to talk really fast. I have to stop him before he says the wrong thing. "Then I—"

I drop my fork on the floor, hoping it looks like an accident.

"Damn it, Sara! Can't you be more careful?" shouts Dad.

"Sorry," I say. "Go ahead, Matt. You were saying you had history tutoring after school."

"Uh-huh," says Zach, without missing a beat. "That's about it."

Dad stands up rather abruptly. "Okay. Everyone hand me your plates." As Dad carries Mom's and Zach's dishes to the counter, I try not to look at the gun.

This is insane. How many days are we going to spend like this, reliving the same meal over and over? We can't rely on Dad to keep us alive. We'll have to get ahold of the gun. *I'll* have to get ahold of the gun. And then—this is where my mind freezes—*If you take the gun, Sara, you have to be ready to use it.*

"Your plate, Sara," Dad holds out his hand expectantly.

"Here, sorry." Flustered, I almost drop my fork again.

Washing the dishes takes Dad about five times as long as it would have taken my mom or me, but it doesn't seem to faze him at all. Each dish is scrubbed carefully, then rinsed. *Front-back-front-back-front.* Drying is *hold-swirl, flip, hold-swirl,* place on counter. *Hold-swirl, flip, hold-swirl,* place on counter. When he's done, he passes the dishcloth around so we can each wipe off our part of the table. Then he sends around the drying towel.

Apparently Zach didn't make the proper number of rotations, because Dad flicks him in the face with the towel and hands it back shouting, "You call that dry?"

Once the dishes are done and the table's cleaned, Dad announces, "Puzzle time! Which one should we do today?" He walks over to the bookcase and pulls down the stack of puzzles. "Mount Rushmore? Forest scene?"

"Is the Statue of Liberty one still there?" Mom asks.

If Dad remembers our trip or smashing the glass statue, he shows no sign. "Statue of Liberty it is." He brings the box to the table and dumps it out in front of us. "Who's doing what? Michelle, you still doing the borders?"

She nods. "Sure."

"Matt and I will do the statue," I volunteer.

We all work quietly. Mom, a little too quickly, as if she's already done the puzzle every day for a week.

"Don't you want to join us, Ray?" Mom asks.

Dad ignores her. Instead of doing the puzzle with us, Dad paces behind us, gun in hand. Each time he passes behind me, I tense, waiting to hear the click of the safety. I start to wonder how much food is left and what Dad will do when we run out. Leaving my mom tied up here alone is one thing, but all three of us? I shake the thought away. We won't be here long enough to run out of food. I'll find us a way out of here before that.

I snap the last piece of the torch into place on the puzzle. The last time we were here, Matt and I had been working on the Niagara Falls puzzle.

"Why don't you try out for the play this year?" Matt asked. "It's always a blast. I can even work it so there are Ritz Bits backstage for you."

"I wouldn't put it past you. But you know I hate people staring at me. Besides, it's much more fun being in the audience watching your shenanigans."

"You're in the band. People stare at you when you're in the band."

"Not really. People are staring at the band; *they don't actually notice the individuals."*

"Whoa there," Matt teased. "Don't go getting all philosophical on me now."

"Oh, please," I said, giving him a little shove.

Dad came in and opened the refrigerator door. "Who put the yogurt in here? It's all over the place. It goes on the second shelf, on the right-hand side. Just like at home. Not scattered all over the whole refrigerator!"

"What the hell's wrong with him?" Matt muttered.

We both knew what Dad would say next. Matt mouthed the words as Dad said them: "And make sure you turn the labels out to the front."

"Sara, I noticed you cleaned the bathroom ahead of schedule. Good

job. Just make sure you keep on top of it, what with all four of us using the same bathroom."

"Wouldn't want to have any water in the shower," Matt muttered. Dad made us wipe the shower walls dry after each use.

"What? Matt, speak up. No keeping secrets!" Dad went to the sink and filled a glass of water. Then he got a paper towel and wiped a drop that had gotten on the floor. "Matt, what are you doing goofing around with that puzzle? I told you to mop this floor first thing this morning!" I followed my dad's gaze to a light footprint by the window. "This floor is filthy! What in God's name were you thinking?"

Don't say it! Whatever you do, don't say it. Just apologize and get right to it.

"That it's only nine o'clock?" Why did Matt always have to make things worse for himself?

Dad gave Matt a shove, and it wasn't at all like the one that I had given him.

I shake my head and try to concentrate on the current puzzle because I don't want to remember all the yelling and Matt's bruises that didn't fade until well after the vacation was over.

"Okay, folks, ten o'clock. Time for bed," Dad announces.

The puzzle is done except for the face of Lady Liberty.

Damn it. I still haven't figured out how to get the gun away from him.

"We've got a lot to do tomorrow."

I can't imagine what.

"Good news, kids. You can go to bed without brushing your

teeth tonight. And without changing into your pajamas. We'll just make a pit stop. You first, Sara." He releases me from the chair, and leads me to the bathroom.

"Can I have some privacy, please?"

Dad wrinkles his forehead. He stares at me uncertainly for a few seconds, then lets go of my hand. "Of course." He backs out of the bathroom and closes the door partway.

This is my chance. What do I do? I turn on the faucet to cover the noise of me opening the medicine cabinet. I find Band-Aids, mouthwash, and a trial size of baby shampoo. Great—there isn't even enough to squirt in his eyes. I look around the rest of the bathroom for a weapon. No razors anywhere—just toilet paper.

With no weapon in sight and no window to escape through, I figure I had better at least use the toilet. I flush. The toilet tank lid! It's large and awkward but also porcelain, perfect for knocking someone out. I taste the adrenaline rushing through my body. I start to lift one side up when the door bangs open. I let the lid slide back into place.

"Okay. Hurry up and wash your hands," says Dad. "You're not the only one who has to go." Before I have a chance to dry my hands, he leads me to one of the bedrooms down the hall. "Take your shoes off and get in."

I lie down on the lumpy mattress. Dad clicks the handcuffs around the slats of the headboard and then ties my feet to the footboard. He has rope everywhere in this place. Then he pulls a musty blanket up to my chin. "Good night, Sara," he says, and kisses me on the forehead. The last time he did that I was probably seven.

Dad disappears for a few minutes and comes back with Zach. He repeats the whole procedure, tying him to the other twin bed and kissing him on the forehead.

"Tomorrow we have to get that gun away from him, Sara," Zach whispers after Dad turns the lights off and leaves. "He's never going to let us go any other way."

"You're right," I say softly. "When one of us sees an opportunity, we'll just do it." I shift my weight, trying to get comfortable.

"I can't believe I was so stupid! I thought Mom was out finding us a new place to live, or that Dad had killed her. I never thought that Dad tied her up in some cabin we don't even own . . . Saturday, when I had Alex driving me around in search of my mom's imaginary lover, I should have thought to look here."

"You're mom's *what?*"

"I found this florist card stuffed in one of my mom's shoes. There was this heart on it and a name. Brian. So Alex and I tracked down some guy my mom used to work with, thinking maybe she was with him."

"Brian?" Zach's voice gets this high-pitched crack in it like when he was back in eighth grade.

"Uh-huh," I say.

Zach turns his face away from me.

"What?"

Zach still won't look at me. "I don't think that card was for your mom."

"What do you mean? Some guy sent flowers to my dad? That would be the day. He'd have flattened him."

Zach clears his throat. "You know the play your brother was in before he—"

"Yeah—"

"Remember the lawyer character?"

"You mean the guy Lauren's brother played? Sure, the character's name was Brian. But what does that have to do with anything? Are you saying that Jay sent the flowers as some kind of a joke?"

"It wasn't a joke."

"Don't be insane. Jay Weston, captain of the basketball team and king of the jocks, sent my brother flowers?"

"Yes." Zach's voice is serious.

"You mean he *liked* my brother?"

"It was more than that."

"Are you saying that Jay and Matt—we're talking about my brother here now—that they were in some kind of relationship?"

Zach clears his throat, but doesn't say anything.

"Goddamn it, Zach. Answer me." Tears trickle out of my eyes. "Unbelievable. You knew? You knew and I didn't?" *I don't believe this, Matt. I am so incredibly pissed at you right now.*

I close my eyes. Dad's voice plays over and over again in my mind. *That goddamned sissy-ass play.* "Is that why Dad wanted him to quit the play so much? Dad knew? And Mom?"

"Yeah," Zach says softly. "Your mom was supportive. But your dad, he said if Matt didn't quit the play and stop seeing Jay, he was going to kick him out of the house. And that he could never come near your mom or you again." Zach swallows hard and shakes his head. "I should have done something. With all that shit your dad said to Matt, I should have known what Matt was going to do. I could have stopped him. Matt would still be alive and your dad wouldn't have flipped out like this."

"Dad started falling apart the minute we left Philly, and you couldn't have known Matt would really—why the hell did he care what Dad thought, anyhow?" But I know the answer. No matter what Dad did to us, no matter how bad he treated us, there was a part of all of us—Mom, Matt, me—that still loved him because of the dad he used to be. A part of each of us still wanted to please him—and wanted him to love us. It's stupid, crazy, and utterly insane. And yet it's still true. "God, Zach, why didn't he tell me?"

I think of my brother leaning against his car. *Need a ride, Sara?*

If I had said yes, would you have told me?

If you had told me, would anything have been any different? Would I have known the right things to stay to stop you from leaving us forever? It's just not what I was expecting. But, hey, sometimes surprises turn out to be the best things about life. I loved *you, Matt. I* loved you for *you. Damn it, Matt, why didn't you stick around?*

"He didn't tell you because he didn't tell anyone, Sara. I only knew because I showed up at your place right after your dad had wailed on him. That was the week before—"

"Matt said he'd fallen down the basement stairs." When Matt had told me, I'd known it was a lie. But I had wanted to believe him. And once again, I'd done nothing. Hadn't told anyone who could have helped. I hadn't even asked why Dad did it. I suppose I had thought that Dad didn't need a reason.

"How come you never told me before, Zach?"

Zach finally looks at me. "I thought it didn't matter anymore." He turns away again. "Or maybe the truth is, it was easier not to tell you."

I have this empty pit in my stomach. How could I not know something this big about my brother's life?

Suddenly I wonder what else I don't know about the people who mean the most to me. "Uh, Zach? You and Matt weren't ever, you know, I mean you're not—"

"Gay? No, Sara, I'm not." Zach sighs.

"Go ahead, say it. This is exactly why Matt didn't tell me. Because I can't even say the word 'gay' out loud."

"I'm sure that isn't the reason, Sara. He knew you would love him no matter what. He was probably just waiting for the right moment."

Like on the bike ride that never was. *Why hadn't I gone?* I make a fist and hit the headboard. *Why?* I hit it again.

"I'm sorry, Sara. I'm no better at dealing with what happened than you are. But I think you'd better stop banging or your Dad's going to come back in here."

"I hope he does. Because then I can—" *Then I can* what, *exactly? Do the same thing I always did when it came to Dad?*

Nothing.

I stop banging and lie perfectly still. "What's that?" The hallway floor creaks under the weight of my dad's footsteps. Is he coming to check on us because of the noise? My stomach clenches. Zach's right. I better pull myself together. There's a belt on the nightstand. My heart pounds. Will Dad hit me with it if he comes in? There's no way I can protect my face. And what if he hits Zach instead of me? Or my mom?

I stay motionless as the seconds tick by. *Thump. Thump.* The footsteps stop outside our door. I hold my breath, as if it'll do any good. Finally the footsteps sound again. I wait another agonizing minute, then let out my breath. He's gone.

"What are we going to do?" I whisper.

Zach stays quiet. I really hope he's thinking of something brilliant.

"We do what he wants for the moment and look for our opportunity. You're our best bet, Sara. You were the only one he left alone in the bathroom. He's the least careful around you. You have to forget what your dad did to Matt and play the part of the obedient daughter."

I clench my fists. "Don't worry. I've been doing that so long, I'd almost forgotten it was a part."

CHAPTER 15

Thursday

I t's not easy to sleep with your arms above your head and your mind filled with images of guns and echoes of your dead brother's voice. The next morning, Dad wakes us up at seven, which feels like it's mere minutes after I've finally fallen asleep. My wrists are numb, my back is sore, and I have to turn my whole body to talk to people because my neck is stiff. And my heart, it's breaking from looking at sweet, brave Zach and my mother's sunken, swollen eyes.

When Dad takes me to the bathroom today, he stands in the doorway, giving me no chance to grab the toilet tank lid as a weapon.

"I need a shower," I say, hoping Dad will leave me unattended. "I always take a shower in the morning."

"Relax," Dad says. "We're camping. It's okay to have a little dirt under your fingernails."

Dad secures us to the kitchen chairs, the same as he did yesterday, leaving one hand free. I'm still the only one whose legs aren't tied.

Breakfast is Cheerios in plastic bowls, both of which I hate. I can't stand the taste or smell of milk in a plastic bowl. The morning is occupied by more puzzles. The Statue of Liberty puzzle has been put away unfinished, but we work on the forest puzzle until we fill in all but the pieces that are missing.

As we work on the puzzle, my mind drifts back to the day Matt died. After I had spent the afternoon making out with Ian and then rehashing the details with Lauren, Jay drove me home like Lauren had told Matt he would. On the ride home, we laughed about how Dan Watkins had fallen into the orchestra pit during the middle of last year's play and how Matt had managed to cover for him by acting like it was part of the show. Now I wonder if Jay had been in such a good mood because he thought he was going to see Matt.

We were still laughing when we walked in the front door. I even forgot to worry about Dad being mad if Jay didn't leave before he got home.

"I Had a Bad Day" was playing on the stereo.

"Not that song again, Matt," I protested. "Turn it off and shoot some hoops with Jay here."

Even though the music was loud, the house was quiet.

"Matt?" That's when I saw the blood. "What's on the—"

Jay tried to cover my eyes, to protect me from seeing what was left of my brother. But it was too late.

*We had stood there together screaming and sobbing in each other's
arms. I thought Jay had been crying from the shock of what we'd just seen.
I hadn't known it was so much more.*

"How about we go for a walk?" suggests Zach. "Remember when we
used to go out walking and collect leaves?"

"No," says Dad. "I don't. I don't think we did." His eyes narrow.
It's as if someone has ripped a hole in Zach's Matt mask. Dad picks
up the gun and turns it over in his hands.

"It was pinecones, Matt. Not leaves," I say.

The hole patches itself. "Right. Pinecones," says Dad.

"Let's go look for pinecones then," I say.

"It's too cold out." Dad's leg twitches nervously. "I know. Reading time!"

I can feel the blood drain from my face. I tossed the Stephen
King book I had "packed" on the front lawn when we left the house.
Dad turns toward the direction of the bedroom, where my duffel
bag is. My palms start to sweat.

One step. Two steps. Three. He hesitates in front of an end
table, then grabs three books.

I feel the color return to my cheeks.

Dad distributes the books at random. I get a Western. Guns
again. My mom, a romance. Zach, a nonfiction book on wild animals. Dad's book is on top of the refrigerator, next to the duct tape.
He takes it down and settles onto the couch. *Surviving Alaska.* It's
the same book he had been reading at home.

* * *

Lunch is two cans of tuna, scooped onto individual plates and served with Saltines. Two pickles each. Tea.

Just as Dad hands Zach a fork, Zach looks at me and nods. *This is it!* We were going to make our move. *You have to get the gun, Sara. You have to do it!* I try not to look at it on the counter. I don't want to make Dad suspicious. Zach takes his fork and stabs it into Dad's arm. Dad jerks away and swings at Zach's face. Zach grabs Dad's arm and holds on.

That's it. That's my cue. I get up and run, dragging my chair behind me. I reach for the gun.

The chair I'm cuffed to yanks back and I fall to the floor. The gun, too. I cringe, expecting it to go off. Zach's also sprawled on the floor and inching toward the gun. But Dad retrieves it in seconds, pulls back the safety, and aims.

At me.

I can't breathe. My whole body trembles. *Don't shoot. Please don't shoot.* I close my eyes tightly, waiting for the boom. I wonder if I'll hear the gunshot before it kills me.

Instead of a bullet, Dad's voice says, "You try anything and I'll shoot her." I open my eyes. Dad is staring coldly at Zach. "And then I'll shoot your mother."

Zach freezes. Dad stares him down for a few more seconds. He puts the gun on the top of the refrigerator, cuffs both of my hands to my chair, and ties my feet. Then Dad cuffs Zach and my mom to their chairs, taking away any freedom we had had.

And with that, lunch is over. For everyone except Dad, that is. He stands at the counter and watches us as he eats his plate of tuna and crackers. He doesn't seem angry, just thoughtful, and I wonder if he's deciding what he's going to do with us.

Dad clears the table, our food untouched. He rinses the dishes but doesn't wash them. Then he dries his hands on the kitchen towel. But when he hangs it on the handle of the oven door, he doesn't straighten it.

Dad plays his guitar all afternoon. He plays the same song fifty times, or maybe it's a hundred. Every so often he picks up the gun which is now on the coffee table in front of him, and flips it over once, twice, three times, then puts it back.

Dinner is the same. Dad eats tuna and crackers while standing at the counter and watching us. We have nothing.

Dad goes back to his guitar after dinner.

When someone finally speaks, it's my mom.

"Ray," she says, in a soothing voice, "the kids need to get back for school tomorrow. Why don't you give the keys to Matt so he and Sara can drive home? Then you and I can enjoy the rest of our vacation here."

What is she doing? Shut up, Mom! There's no way he'll let us go. She's just going to make him angry.

"This is a family vacation, Michelle. We should all be together. Aren't you having a good time, Sara?" No mention of how we'd tried to escape.

I nod and try to smile.

"What? Speak up!"

"Yes, of course. It's great."

"Matt?"

"Sure Dad."

"See, Michelle? They want to be here."

"But Sara has a history test and Matt has play rehearsal." Mom's voice is strong.

Dad leans his guitar against the coffee table. The strings buzz. Dad glares at me. "Didn't you tell me that Matt quit the play?" Dad asks. "Huh? Isn't that what you said, Sara?"

"I—uh, yes, of course he quit," I say. "Mom just didn't know yet."

Dad takes the gun from the coffee table and crosses the room to tower over Zach.

"Did you quit the play or not? Look at me when I'm talking to you!"

"Yeah, I quit. Just like you wanted."

"Don't lie to me!" Dad slaps Zach across the face.

Dad seems especially agitated. A bad feeling spreads through me. Something feels different. Like Dad's about to snap. *I have to do something, and fast.*

"Stop it, Dad!" I shout. "That's not Matt, it's Zach! Matt is dead!"

Dad turns toward me. But the blank look in his eyes tells me that he hasn't processed what I said. Or that he doesn't want to.

"Come on, Sara, let's go," Dad says, cold and matter-of-fact. He unties my legs and unlocks my handcuffs.

"Dad?" My voice sounds shrill to my own ears. "You know that's not Matt. It's Zach. Let him go home!"

"Mr. Peters," Zach pleads. "I'm sorry I let you think I'm Matt. Can't we all stay here and figure things out together?"

"Ray!"

My dad, his face expressionless, doesn't answer. Instead he drags me out to the camper, opens the door, and pushes me in the back.

I try again, pleading in my quiet voice. "It's Zach, Dad. It's Zach."

"Get under the table," Dad barks. He cuffs me around the table leg again.

God, what's happening? Does Dad understand what I told him? Does he know that it's Zach inside the cabin and not Matt?

Dad slams the camper door behind him.

"Dad!" Panic overwhelms me. *Where is he taking me?* But Dad doesn't climb in the front seat of the camper. Is he going to bring Mom and Zach along? Or is he going to hurt them? My blood turns ice-cold.

I pull at my handcuffs, then stop. A weird feeling crawls through me. Something is different about the camper. Something *smells* different. I'm sure of it. I shake my head. *God, I'm getting to be just as crazy as my dad. I have to stop imagining things!*

Then a whisper, "Sara!"

My heart stops. "Alex?"

The bathroom door creaks open.

"Oh my God, Alex. Are you really here?" I'm horribly afraid that my mind is playing tricks on me.

"I'm really here." Alex crawls to the table and hugs me.

"I can't believe you came." I start crying, both from relief that Alex is here and fear about what is going on inside the cabin.

"Where's the key to those?" he says, gesturing at the handcuffs.

"There's one in the cabin, but Dad had another one out here. I saw him put it in that top drawer when he took me in—then he came back out for Zach, so he might have moved it." *Or put it in his pocket.* "Did you call for help?" I ask hopefully.

Alex shakes his head as he begins rummaging through the drawer. "No service. And I didn't tell anyone where I was going because I wasn't sure what to expect—whether you needed help or you were just running away with Zach."

"With Zach?" I'm completely confused. "Didn't you find the page from *Soap Opera Digest*?"

Alex starts tossing things out of the drawer—flashlight, batteries. "The thing about the Julia girl being pregnant?"

"Pregnant? What?"

"I thought that was what this whole thing was about. You've looked kind of sick and upset lately, and you've been meeting Zach every day, like the two of you are sharing some sort of secret—I thought you were pregnant."

"No, not pregnant. Definitely not pregnant. But my dad—he's lost it. He thinks Zach is Matt."

"Holy shit. As soon as I find the key and can get you free, I want you to take my car and get out of here as fast as you can. I parked by the end of the driveway, just around the corner. Here are my keys." He tosses them next to me.

Bam! A single gunshot.

I scream, choke, and cry. Alex freezes. I cringe, bracing for a second. Nothing.

Slam! Alex peers cautiously out of the window. "That's the cabin door. Your dad has Zach, but he looks okay." Alex sounds relieved.

"My mom is in there too," I whisper. *Please, God, no! Please let it just have been a warning shot.*

"Jesus." Alex's eyes widen. "Hang in there, Sara. We'll get to her. Where the hell is that key?" Alex glances out the window again. "Your dad's taking Zach behind the cabin."

My heart pounds. "There's only one thing behind the cabin. The river."

Alex yanks out the next drawer and dumps it out. I hear a tinkling sound as the contents hit the floor.

"That's it!" I say.

Alex pats his hands across the floor. "Where did it go? I lost it!"

"Over there, by the stove. Hurry!"

Alex grabs the key. His hands are shaking so hard, it takes several tries to open the lock.

Finally I'm free. Alex and I scramble down the stairs. "Go help your mom. Here, take the key," Alex says. "I'll go after your Dad and Zach."

"But—"What if he can't handle Dad on his own? And what if I can't handle what I might see in the cabin? Images of the way I had found Matt's body flash through my mind. *No.*

"Go, Sara! See if she needs help, then meet me behind the cabin."

I nod and take off running. *Please let her be okay.*

On the porch, I yank open the cabin door, my heart thudding in my ears.

Red. Blood. On the floor.

It's Matt all over again. Bleeding. Dying. Dead.

"Mom!"

She's curled up on the floor, eyes closed.

No! It isn't supposed to happen like this. We were going to get away. It can't end like this.

My knees feel weak, as if I'm about to collapse.

A soft moan.

She's alive.

I hurry toward Mom. She clutches her right leg on both sides, just above the ankle. Blood seeps between her fingers.

"I'm here, Mom."

"He untied me. I—tried—to—run—"

"Shh," I say gently. "Don't talk."

Think! What did my guidebook say about gunshot wounds? I reach for the towel on the oven door. *No. Try to find something clean.* I yank open the drawer where the clean dish towels are kept.

"Here, use these," I say, slipping the towels between her fingers and the wounds, one on each side of her leg. *Entrance. Exit.* "Try to put pressure on them."

"Don't—run—he—said—don't—run."

"It's okay, Mom. Everything's going to be okay." Despite my own terror, I know I need to keep her calm. *I already lost you once, Mom. I can't lose you again.* "Stay with me, Mom."

I need something to keep the towels in place in case my mom passes out. *Rope? Duct tape.*

"I'll be right back. I'm just going to get something from the kitchen. You're doing great."

Matt, help me here. Help me save Mom.

I murmur reassurances as I wrap the duct tape around the towels, securing them.

Elevate. You're supposed to elevate, Sara.

I snatch a pillow from the couch and slide it under Mom's leg. Then I stroke her face. "You're going to be fine. Everything's going to be just fine."

Bam! A gunshot sounds from outside. *No. No. No. Now who has he hurt? I have to go help! But how can I leave Mom?*

"Go," she murmurs. "Go."

Summoning every last ounce of courage, I stagger out of the cabin.

I need a weapon. Something I can use to stop Dad. I look for a tool, a branch, anything. *Do I go back into the cabin to get a knife? If I did, could I use it?*

The storage chest.

I bound down the cabin stairs and over to the storage chest. Whipping open the cover, I start flinging water toys across the lawn until I find something I can use: a canoe paddle.

I round the corner. A few yards away near the riverbank, Alex is on the ground. Dad kicks him. Over and over again. I want to scream and make him stop, but I need to catch Dad off guard.

Where is Zach? And where is the gun? It has to be nearby, but I don't see it. I charge.

I swing the paddle back and aim for Dad. I cringe as I do it, not wanting to hurt him, even after all that he's done. It knocks him to the ground, but only for a second. He pushes himself up and starts in my direction.

I swing again, but Dad grabs the paddle and wrenches it away from me. He turns it sideways and raises it over his head.

I'm frozen in terror. At the last second, I move. Instead of smashing into my skull, the paddle slices into my shoulder. I scream and double over in pain.

Dad kicks me in the side. He raises the paddle again. I roll out of the way just as Alex, crawling up behind Dad, grabs both of his feet and knocks him down next to me. *Where the hell is Zach?*

"Gun—over—there," Alex gasps.

I scramble toward it. Dad grabs my pants leg. I stumble, but break free of Dad's hold. There it is, lying in front of me, daring me to pick it up. I want to get up and run, but Alex needs me. And Mom. And Zach, wherever he is.

I grab the gun.

The moment I touch it, I see my brother. A thousand images of him flash in an instant, only two of which I can see clearly: him leaning against his convertible—*Coming, Sara?*—and him lying dead on the dining room floor.

There's a grunt behind me. It's Dad. He's on top of Alex, his hands around Alex's neck. Pressing, squeezing, forcing the life out of him. Like he'd done to my family, over and over again.

"Stop!" I shout. "I have the gun! You have to let him go! He's choking!" The gun feels cold and heavy. My hands shake. There's no way I can do this.

Dad looks at me for a second, but he doesn't stop. He knows I won't do anything. I never do.

There's a ringing in my ears, blocking out all other sounds.

I know how to aim a gun. I'm a cop's daughter, after all. Dad taught me how to shoot way before he ever became the enemy.

"Stop! I'm counting to three! Please, don't make me do this," I beg, tears streaming down my face.

Stop the shaking. You have to stop your hands from shaking. Alex is going to die if you don't.

I remember the first time I jumped into deep water. I had been so terrified, my whole body shook. And then Matt had taken my hand. *I need you now, Matt. I really need you.*

"One." I can hear the difference in my own voice and my trembling subsides.

"Two. I'm not kidding, Dad." He must know I mean it. I can see it in his eyes as he looks up at me. For a moment, I see the sweet dad who gave me Sam. But then there's nothing but coldness.

"Three."

Alex tries to pry Dad's hands off his neck. Instead of stopping, Dad squeezes harder. Alex's hands go limp.

The roar of the river fills my ears.

"Daddy!" I scream.

I squeeze the trigger.

He lets go.

I sob and fall to my knees, knowing I'll never have the will to get up again.

Daddy. Daddy, what have I done?

Alex, coughing, crawls out from underneath Dad's body.

"Zach," says Alex, his voice barely a whisper. He points to the river.

There is no way Zach is still alive in that water.

How can I even find him? Everything is a fog. Besides, I can't get up. I'm never getting up again.

Come on, Sara, get up! You have to try.

"Is he shot?"

"In the leg," Alex croaks. It makes sense. *Don't run* is what Mom said Dad had told her. I get a lump in my throat as I think about how Dad didn't want us to leave him, no matter what the cost.

"Mom's in the—Mom—cabin." I'm trembling so much that I can barely get the words out. And my thoughts are swirling so, I'm not sure that the words coming out make any sense. "I'm—Zach—going."

I stumble over to the river, ditch my shoes, and jump in.

God, it's cold! How long has Zach been in here? I have a horrible feeling that I am way, way too late.

Where is he, Matt? You've got to help me find him, I think frantically.

I let the current pull me, using my hands to feel under the water for Zach. Nothing.

"Zach!" I know it's pointless, but I scream his name over and over again. I dive down, opening my eyes under the water, but see nothing.

As I come up for air, I slam my head into a fallen log. With no chance to take a breath, I'm back under, inhaling water through my nose. I open my mouth from the shock and more water rushes in.

I feel like I'm stuck in my horrible oatmeal dream. *So this is what it feels like to drown.* I panic, kicking as hard as I can.

I break the surface, coughing, choking, gagging. I cling to the log and rest. *I can't do this anymore!*

Yes, you can. You have to—Zach is running out of time.

I push off from the log and swim around it. *I have to get back and help Mom. It's too late for Zach. I've got to get back to Mom.*

Another fallen tree blocks the river, but there's something snagged on it. *Zach's handcuffs!*

"Zach! Hold on, I'm coming!"

With every stroke, I strain to reach as far as I possibly can to get to him faster.

"Zach!" I shake him. He doesn't answer. *Damn it! How am I going to get him back to the shore?* I can try to pull him up onto the log, but even if I manage to lift him, the log leads to the wrong side of the riverbank. I'm going to have to swim with him. Doubt nags at me. I'm a horrible swimmer.

Snap out of it, Sara. This isn't gym class. This is Zach's life. You can do it.

I try to pull him so that his hands will come free of the log, but I'm working against the current and trying to tread water. My strength is fading. I swing my feet to push off against the trunk. I try again.

Snap! Suddenly I have the full weight of Zach's body in my arms. Water pours into my mouth and nose. We're sinking. Down. Down. Down. With one hand wrapped around Zach, I kick my feet and try to swim upward.

Don't let go. Need air. Don't let go. Need air. Don't. Let. Go.

It's no use. I can't swim and hold on to Zach. But I won't let him go. I couldn't save my brother but I can save Zach.

Buzzing. A fly? I'm losing it. I must be dying.

Don't let go!

Kick!

Harder!

Adrenaline surges through my body and I make another push for the surface.

Air! Finally air! Coughing, choking. It doesn't matter. *Air!*

Something bumps my arm.

"Sara! The ring." It's Alex's voice, but quiet and raspy.

I have to get to Alex. I grab the life preserver and slide it under Zach's head. I scoop with my left hand, pulling Zach along with my right, with a speed unlike any I've ever had in gym class. *Kick. Scoop. Pull. Kick, kick, kick. Almost there. Scoop. Pull. Kick.*

The shore. Kneeling on the bank, Alex reaches into the water and seizes my hand, bringing us closer. I grab a rock and scramble out of the water while Alex steadies the life preserver with Zach.

Alex slides an arm under one of Zach's armpits and motions for me to do the same. Together, we draw Zach out of the water, laying him down on the muddy bank.

Damn it. His leg is bleeding.

Alex puts two fingers on the side of Zach's neck. "He's got a pulse," he whispers. He bends down and puts his ear by Zach's mouth. He shakes his head. "He's not breathing."

My stomach drops.

Come on, Zach, you can't leave me.

Ninth-grade health class. All I can remember are plastic CPR dummies and the overpowering scent of bleach. I latch on to the memory of the smell, and I can feel myself back in the classroom, kneeling on the floor, leaning over the body . . .

Airway.

Head back, chin up, nose pinched.

Breathe. I touch Zach's cool skin and feel the panic sliding around inside of me. I touch my lips to his and breathe. Tears prick my eyes. I don't know what I'm doing. This isn't working. *Come on, Zach, come on.* Again. *You can't die on me, Zach. You can't.*

Three.

It's too late. This isn't helping.

Four.

His body twitches. Coughs. Heaves.

Alex and I roll Zach to his side. Water gushes out. His eyes open.

"Zach!" I press my face against his cheek.

Alex takes off his shirt and ties it around Zach's leg. "I'll go get the camper," Alex says.

Dread fills me. "But the keys . . . Dad . . ."

I can't look at Dad's body. There's no way I can get the keys out of his pocket. *If I don't look, maybe it won't be real.*

"Got it covered," says Alex softly, holding up a key chain labeled in Dad's neat handwriting. He takes off running.

The camper rumbles to life and bounces its way through the dirt toward us. Alex jumps out of the cab, leaving the engine running and the door open. "Now comes the hard part," he says.

As Alex carries Zach to the camper, I hold his leg to keep it from banging against the stairs. Zach groans in pain. I flinch, wishing there was something more I could do.

"Hold on," I say, slamming the door shut with Zach and Alex inside. I climb into the cab of the camper, throw it in gear, and pull up to the door of the cabin. I race up the stairs, worry surging through my veins.

"Mom?"

She doesn't answer, but her eyelids flutter. Alex scoops her up like he did Zach.

"I'll ride back here with them," I say. "Do you know how to get out of here?"

"We'll soon find out," Alex answers.

For once I'm glad that he drives fast.

In the hospital waiting room Alex wraps his arms around me and rocks me, holding on like he'll never let go.

A hospital volunteer asks if there's anything she can do for us. We tell her about Dad.

We also give her names to call, and one by one, people arrive. Zach's parents first. I'm afraid they'll hate me. Instead, they hug me and they say they wish they had known.

Zach's mother holds my left hand and Alex my right. And this is how we wait.

Alex's parents are there too. I like them. They look like people who linked pinkies in high school and never stopped being in love. And I can't help thinking that maybe Alex and I will look like that someday.

Then Jay walks in and we cry in each other's arms once again. This time I whisper, "I'm glad he picked you."

For a moment he's frozen. Then he holds me even closer. "Thanks," he says. "Me too."

Lauren buys me Ritz Bits from the vending machine. I can't eat them, but she says to hold on to them for later.

I feel love all around me, here in this room. So different from being with Dad.

When the doctors walk in, hours later, I try to read their faces. But I can't. The heavy scent of disinfectant clings to the walls and smothers me with fear.

"They're . . ." The room spins and I squeeze Alex's hand.

". . . going to make it."

The next day Mom and I watch *The Winds of Change* in her hospital room. Julia finally figures out the truth about Ramón. Mom says

she's done watching the show. She likes how Julia and her real husband are finally back together and happy. That's the way she wants
to remember them. I agree.

I sit right next to Mom, holding tightly to her hand, even
though I know she's not going anywhere. She's thin, too thin. I
didn't see that at the cabin, but I see it now. The IV drips steadily
into her, and I prod her to take a bite of the turkey sandwich that
I've saved from her lunch plate.

She tugs at the sleeve of her hospital gown, trying to pull it over
a bruise. "You're not going home alone, are you?" Mom asks, looking
worried. .

"No. I'm staying with Jay and Lauren," I say. "Until Grandma
and Grandpa get here."

She nods and smiles, and her eyes drift closed.

That night I have the oatmeal dream.
    Only it's not me who's drowning.
    It's my dad. And I can't save him.
    I wake up with tears on my pillow.

The cops have all been the very opposite of Jack Reynolds. *No
charges will be filed,* they tell me.
    Don't worry, I almost say.
    My heart is in its own prison.
    A father should never have to bury his own son.
    And a daughter should never have to do what I've done.
    Every time I reach for something, I remember the feel of the gun.

Every time I close my eyes, I remember squeezing the trigger.
Every time I open them, I remember seeing you lying there, Dad.
I will never forget.
And my stupid, stupid, heart will never stop loving you.

I walk into Zach's room. Lauren is there. *Again.* I see a sparkle in Zach's eyes. The same one I see when Alex looks at me. I laugh as I finally get it.

"What? What's so funny?" asks Lauren.

"Oh, nothing," I say innocently. I turn to Zach. "When are you getting out of here?"

"This afternoon," Zach and Lauren say together.

They both blush.

"And your mom?" asks Zach.

"She's filling out the paperwork now."

I say good-bye and head down to my mom's room. The nurse helps me get her into the wheelchair, and I hand Mom a couple of plants to hold on her lap.

I wheel Mom down the hallway and out the automatic doors of the hospital. It's cool out, but there's a hint of sun in the sky. A train whistle blows and suddenly I'm five again and Matt and I are riding on a steam train, our heads sticking out the window, flakes of soot hitting our hair, laughing. Dad is there with us, happy too.

As the whistle fades I'm left here, but in my mind the train goes on, my brother and Dad riding together, and I wave good-bye.

Alex pulls up to the curb. He opens the door for Mom, and I

help her in. As Alex walks back around to the driver's side, I reach over and click her seat belt.

"You did what you had to do," she whispers. "I only wish I could have done it for you."

"I know," I say. I put my hand on her shoulder. "I know you do. Let's go home."

Acknowledgments

I would like to give a huge thank-you to the following people:

My editor, Annette Pollert, who is incredibly supportive and amazes me with her attention to detail.

Anica Rissi, Guillian Helm, and the entire Simon Pulse team.

My agent, Kevan Lyon, who is an awesome cheerleader and who always gets right back to me.

Jill Marsal for the question that inspired a new direction for this book.

My SCBWI-MI mentor, Shutta Crum, for her wonderful suggestions and all the things she taught me.

John Snider and Rick McLatcher for answering my medical and police questions (any errors are mine, not theirs).

The many people who read drafts of this book, especially critique partners Kristin Lenz, Lisa Chottiner, and Gina Miller.

All my great friends at YA Fusion, the Apocalypsies, SCBWI-MI, GDRWA, and YARWA.

The writing teachers who inspired and encouraged me: Gloria Kempton, Mark Spencer, Joan Bartlett, Dee Burt, Carol Wyman, John Mohn, Dr. Richard Koch, and Dr. Carol Leventen.

Millie J. Ragosta, the author I met when I was a teen, who shared galleys of her books and other cool writer things with me.

The colleagues who answered my random questions in the halls and my students who were so supportive.

My "Library Mom," Leona Harland.

My husband (who brought me snacks as I worked on edits) and my mom, who encouraged me along the way.

And my kids for understanding when Mom couldn't play because she was working on her book!

About the Author

Tracy Bilen is a high school French and Spanish teacher. She lives in Michigan with her husband and two children.

From *New York Times* bestselling author

LISA McMANN

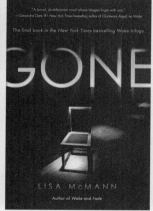

lisamcmann.com

living

dead

girl

A NOVEL

"Stark. Gripping. Totally unforgettable."
—Ellen Hopkins, author of *CRANK*

ELIZABETH SCOTT

Once upon a time,
I **did not** live in Shady Pines.

Once upon a time,
my name **was not** Alice.

Once upon a time,
I didn't know how lucky **I was**.

FROM SIMON PULSE | PUBLISHED BY SIMON & SCHUSTER

Girls you like. Emotions you know. Outcomes that make you think.

ALL BY

DEBCALETTI

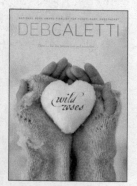

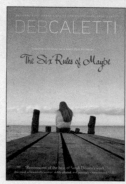

EBOOK EDITIONS ALSO AVAILABLE

FROM SIMONPULSE TEEN.SimonandSchuster.com

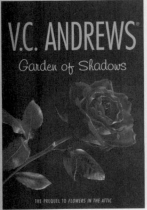
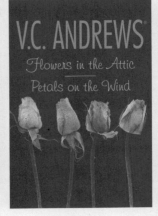

YOU ALWAYS HURT
THE ONE YOU LOVE.

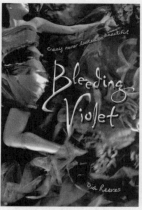

The road less traveled might just be the ride of your life!

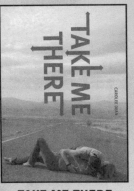

TAKE ME THERE
Carolee Dean

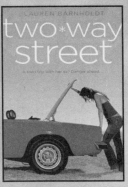

TWO-WAY STREET
Lauren Barnholdt

CRASH INTO ME
Albert Borris

DRIVE ME CRAZY
Erin Downing

THE MISSION
Jason Myers

SiMONTEEN

Simon & Schuster's **Simon Teen**
e-newsletter delivers current updates on
the hottest titles, exciting sweepstakes, and
exclusive content from your favorite authors.

Visit **TEEN.SimonandSchuster.com** to
sign up, post your thoughts, and find out what
every avid reader is talking about!